JAN 2009

WARRICK'S BATTLE

Haunted by the past, Paul Warrick is assailed by bad memories, and in an attempt to forget, drifts from town to town finding work. But a shoot-out at a casino lands him in jail, and with the valley on the verge of a range war, Paul's actions might be the fire to light the fuse. Paul becomes involved in the final show-down — and he must not only save his life, but also his own sanity at the same time!

TERRELL L. BOWERS

WARRICK'S BATTLE

Complete and Unabridged

LINFORD
Leicester

First published in Great Britain in 2007 by
Robert Hale Limited
London

First Linford Edition
published 2008
by arrangement with
Robert Hale Limited
London

British Library CIP Data

Bowers, Terrell L.
    Warrick's battle.—Large print ed.—
Linford western library
    1. Western stories
    2. Large type books
    I. Title
    813.5′4 [F]

    ISBN 978–1–84782–468–4

Published by
F. A. Thorpe (Publishing)
Anstey, Leicestershire

Set by Words & Graphics Ltd.
Anstey, Leicestershire
Printed and bound in Great Britain by
T. J. International Ltd., Padstow, Cornwall

This book is printed on acid-free paper

1

The job at Joker's Wild saloon and casino wasn't great but it paid decent wages. Paul Warrick had wandered into Liberty, Wyoming and asked about work. A couple of nights later he had himself a new profession. He ran a faro table six nights a week from dusk till dawn. Going to bed shortly before sun-up, he usually experienced an exhausted, dreamless sleep, the best kind for a man with his past. It didn't pay to get too rested or the mind would begin to conjure up vivid images from days gone by.

Paul played a square game knowing the odds were on his side and regularly won a fair amount for the house. Along with the usual winnings he had also passed along a gold watch, a diamond tie-stud, a couple horses and the deed to a small farm.

After a couple weeks, he learned to recognize the sort of man who stepped up to his faro table. The timid sort usually placed a meager bet or two and quit when they lost. Others would play a set amount until they were broke. The worst were the compulsive gamblers, men who refused to quit. They played until they lost their last nickel, then borrowed from friends to continue . . . until they ran out of friends. The occasional player who was fortunate enough to end up winning would often move on to other games of chance to try their luck. Professional gamblers who visited the casino sat down to poker or blackjack, where they had better odds of leaving the table ahead of the game. Paul quickly learned the unspoken rule concerning games of chance — men who gambled against the house rarely left a winner.

It was an all right occupation, other than when playing the kind of man who didn't know when to quit. For them, gambling was an aggressive disease, an illness which took control of their mind and soul. It stripped their thinking process of logic. After losing a portion of their money they would begin to play in desperation to win back their stake. In the end they usually left entirely broke. Most men took the loss in their stride, accepting blame for their own misfortune. Occasionally, an obstinate player took losing as a personal insult.

The gent standing across from him was such a man. Ned Calloway had been drinking. He usually came in with one of his brothers or cousins. Tonight he was alone and he definitely needed someone to watch over him. Ned had started with over a hundred dollars in his pockets, but he bet and played recklessly. He threw money down like it was too hot to hold in his hand. After thirty minutes he was frustrated, surly and had his last dollar on the table.

'You're a dirty, low-down cheat, Warrick!' he snarled, when his card did not come up for the last time. 'Ain't no one that lucky!'

Paul swept the money from the table to the dealer's drawer. He remained poised and spoke calmly. 'You've been betting hog wild tonight, Ned. A blind man could have taken your money.'

But Ned backed up a step and menacingly placed his hand on his gun. 'I'm sayin' you're a liar and a cheat!' he bellowed. 'Gimme back my money or I'll gut shoot yuh here and now!'

The dealer's drawer was open. Paul kept a short-barrel .32 caliber pistol next to his cash box. Hidden from view by the top of the table, he rested his hand on the gun.

'I don't want any trouble, Ned.' He kept his voice passionless. 'If you've got a complaint, talk to Gastone.'

Mort Gastone was owner of the Joker's Wild casino and had earned a reputation as a hard man. Getting a dime out of him was like trying to squeeze lemon juice from a railroad spike.

'Gastone warn't the man who done took my money,' Ned growled.

The veins on his forehead stood out against his flushed face and his teeth were firmly set. Too much liquor added to his mounting fury. Paul observed the knuckles on Ned's gun hand were white from the pressure of his grip on the butt of his Colt. He was spoiling for a fight.

Paul attempted to defuse the situation. 'How about I give you twenty dollars credit and you try your luck at another table?'

'I'm takin' back every dollar yuh took from me, Warrick.' Ned slurred his words, but there was murder in his eyes. 'Time for you to meet your Maker!'

Ned yanked the gun from its holster, thumb-cocking the hammer, clearing leather instantly. He was drunk but his speed was still deadly.

Paul hastily whipped the pistol from the cash drawer — it cleared the table top at chest level — and fired before Ned could squeeze the trigger on his own gun.

The suddenness of a foreign object

entering Ned's chest stopped him in mid-motion. His face skewed, displaying a mixture of shock and disbelief. He had mistakenly thought Paul would have to reach for a gun on his hip. He figured to beat the faro dealer with ease. Stunned, he took a step back, but abruptly lacked the strength to stand. He sagged to his knees and gazed in wonder at the tiny hole in his shirt front.

'If that don't beat all!' he muttered. 'Shot by some double-dealing dude!' Then he toppled over onto his back.

Paul placed the gun back down in the drawer and came around from the table. A crowd gathered about as he knelt down to check Ned's wound. It took only a glance to see that his defensive and hurried aim had scored a fatal hit. The man's eyes were wide open, but the light of consciousness had left his body. Ned Calloway was dead.

Dodge Roper, the town sheriff, arrived moments after the shooting. Agewise, he was on the far side of forty, but at over six feet and a solid 200 pounds, he still possessed the bulk and stature to command respect. He wasted no time taking charge.

'A couple of you boys grab hold of Ned and carry his body over to Hadley's place.' Kip Hadley was his part-time deputy, a carpenter and sign-maker. He also acted as town mortician in that he would help prepare a lost soul for his final rest at the Liberty cemetery. Dodge waved a pointed finger at several men. 'One of you boys better ride out and tell Buford.'

'He ain't gonna be happy to hear his boy is dead,' a man sounded off.

'Tell him I've got the man who done it behind bars,' Dodge told him firmly. 'I don't want him thinking he and his boys can come gunning for Warrick.'

'I'll pass the word,' one man offered. 'I seen a couple of the Calloway wranglers over at the café. Be safer if we let them take the news. Save risking a chance that one of the Calloways might do harm to the messenger!'

Mort Gastone pushed through the circle of men and planted himself opposite the sheriff. 'You can't arrest Warrick,' he barked, placing his hands on his hips and thrusting out his jaw. 'I seen the whole thing from across the room. Ned drew down on my dealer. He had to defend himself or be killed.'

Several other men began to voice the same story.

Dodge held up both hands, palms out, to stop the chatter. Soon as he had silence, he nodded to the saloon owner.

'Collect your money from the faro table, Gastone,' he told him steadfastly. 'This young feller won't be dealing for you any more tonight.'

Paul surrendered the gun from his cash drawer and went without protest. When they reached the town jail, he entered the only cell and sat down on one of the two cots.

'Mort told the truth, Sheriff,' he explained quietly. 'Ned wouldn't be talked out of a gunfight. He drew his gun and I had to shoot him or be killed.'

Dodge closed the cell door. 'I don't doubt your story, Warrick. Ned is the wildest . . . *was* the wildest of the entire Calloway bunch. We've been nurse-maiding a likely range war betwixt the farmers and the ranchers for the past couple years. I've been expecting someone from one side or the other to end up dead. It's a real surprise to have it be a faro dealer who done the killing.'

'If you believe it was a fair fight, why am I in jail?'

'You want to get shot full of holes?' Dodge threw the words at him. 'How long do you think you'd live with the Calloway clan out to get your hide?' He snorted. 'You'd have a better chance against hell's fury, son. If I didn't arrest you, them Calloways would string you from the nearest tree before sunrise.'

Paul showed a crooked grin. 'There isn't a decent-sized tree for ten miles in any direction, Sheriff.'

'Those Calloways would sure enough build one!'

'So incarceration is what — a measure of protective guardianship for my own safety?'

'Fancy way of saying it, but yeah. The Calloways know me. They know I won't let no one be taken from my jail. I'm betting they will let you live through the night, so long as I'm right here to watch over you.'

'And what if they come in force to take me?'

Rather than answer immediately, Dodge heaved his massive chest and rested his haunch on the corner of his desk. 'I'm about to become a grandfather, Warrick,' he said softly, his face revealing an inner tenderness. 'My daughter, Sarah, is due to have her baby any day now. I'd hate like hell to end up dead before I set eyes on my grandchild.'

'Nix to that,' Paul responded. 'If it comes down to getting yourself killed to protect me, you just open the cell door and let me deal with Ned's relatives.'

Dodge frowned. 'You would sure enough end up on the underside of several feet of dirt, son. I can't believe you take life so casual.'

Paul uttered a sigh. 'There are things I've done and witnessed, Sheriff — more than a man should see.' Paul slowly turned his head from side to side. 'I haven't had a peaceful night's sleep in a good many years. I believe dying is probably the only escape I will ever have from reality.'

'That's crazy talk!' Dodge snapped. 'I'd wager you ain't more'n twenty-five years old!'

'Twenty-seven,' Paul corrected, 'but it's not the years, it's the deeds, the ghastly memories, the knowledge of man's inhumanity to man. It consumes a person's soul until he longs for relief . . . even death.'

Dodge opened his mouth but a pounding at the door prevented further comment.

He whirled about, pulled his gun and

stepped over to ease open the door. Kip Hadley stood there, panting for breath, a fretful expression on his face. It was obvious the man had not brought good news.

'What the devil, Kip?' Dodge demanded sourly. 'Since when do you have to knock. You're my deputy for crying out loud!'

'I was thinking how you might be sitting with your Greener pointed at the door, Sheriff,' he huffed. 'Wasn't of a mind to catch a load of buckshot from that shotgun before you realized it was me.'

'What are you doing here? Don't you have a body to look after?'

'Bryan seen the light at my workshop and run over from his place,' he gasped, still breathing hard. 'Your daughter is suffering terrible labor, but the midwife can't deliver the baby. Martha told him that Sarah and the baby are both going to die!'

Dodge staggered back a step, the news hitting him like a sudden punch to his jaw. He shoved his gun back into its holster and grabbed the corner of his desk for support.

'No!' he lamented, instantly choked with emotion. 'Not my little girl.'

'Bryan said at first they thought the baby was breech,' Kip hurried on with the report, 'but now the midwife says the baby can't come. Sarah is in real bad pain and there's nothing Martha can do!' He gave a sad shake of his head. 'Bryan said you best not waste any time getting there.'

Dodge straightened up and took a step toward the door, before he remembered his prisoner. 'I can't leave Warrick in here by himself. One of the Calloway boys might show up at any moment. They would shoot him in his cell.'

'I'll stay,' Kip offered. 'This could be your only chance to say goodbye!'

Dodge gulped back his emotion. 'I can't ask you to risk your life by — '

'I'll go with you,' Paul interrupted Dodge. When the sheriff turned his head to look at him he said: 'Maybe I can be of some help.'

Dodge did not hide his incredulity. 'You? You can help my girl?'

'I know a little about medicine,' Paul admitted softly.

'Are you a doctor of some kind?'

Paul shrugged his shoulders. 'I used to be . . . a lifetime ago. I have a medical bag in my room at the boarding-house.'

'Do you think there's a chance?' Dodge asked, obviously afraid to let hope enter his voice.

'I don't know, Sheriff, but we have no time to lose. If she's in hard labor every second counts.'

'You go fetch his bag, Kip,' Dodge ordered. 'Do it now!'

'Room Four, under the bed, a black valise,' Paul informed him.

Kip took off running while Dodge fumbled with the cell key. It eventually turned in the lock and he took a moment to study Paul. There was a desperate longing etched into his features as he searched for a glimmer of hope.

'She's my only child, Warrick.' His voice cracked from the strain and tears glistened in his eyes. He swung open the door and pleaded: 'If you can do anything . . .'

'We'd better hurry,' Paul suggested. 'If the baby is in peril, we might already be too late.'

They went out the door, sprinted down the street and turned up the alley between the general store and the bakery. Bryan had a modest three-room cottage a short distance from his store.

When they reached the house, Dodge pushed through the front door with Paul right on his heels.

Bryan stood at the bedside, shoulders sagging, as if he was suffering the weight of the world. His expression, when he looked at them, displayed a mixture of unbearable dread and grief. A few feet from him, the midwife, a woman well past her child-bearing years, was at the foot of the bed. Tears wet her cheeks while she wrung her hands and shook her

15

head from side to side.

'It's no use!' she sobbed. 'The baby can't come. There's nothing I can do!'

Paul put his attention on the pregnant woman. Sarah was drenched in sweat, her eyes wide with pain and fright. She gasped for every breath, fighting the ache of contractions and agonizing over the prospect of impending death for both herself and her child.

Paul moved over to the bed at once. He was breathing hard from the run, but mustered forth an outward professional calm and placed a hand on the woman's brow.

'Take it easy, Sarah,' he spoke gently, looking directly into her eyes, 'it's going to be all right.' It took a moment before her eyes actually focused on him. When he felt certain she could hear him, he began to instruct her.

'Sarah, take a couple deep breaths and let them out slowly. I need for you to be calm and try to relax.'

Sarah, somewhat reassured by his tone of voice and composure, gulped a swallow of air and struggled to curb a measure of her fear and panic.

'Can you feel the baby?' Paul asked gently. 'Is he still moving?'

'I . . . I . . . ' She battled valiantly to suppress her terror. 'I can't tell.'

Paul laid his head down with his ear pressed to her abdomen. The room fell silent and he thought he could detect two heart beats — mother and child.

'I'll need hot water and towels!' he directed the midwife. 'Also, find me a clean sheet or something we can cut up for a bandage. Hurry!'

The midwife stared at him blankly.

'Go!' Dodge bellowed at her. 'Heat some water.' Then turning to Bryan, he ordered: 'Bring the other things he needs.'

Bryan took a step, stopped and arched his eyebrows when he took a closer look at Paul. 'Isn't that the fellow who deals at one of the faro tables?'

'Just get something to use as a clean bandage,' Dodge instructed him. 'Make it quick!'

The woman had scampered over to the sink and dumped a container of drinking water into a pan. She had it on the stove and heating by the time Bryan had found a clean sheet.

Kip arrived with Paul's medical bag a minute or two later. He was completely spent from the hard run.

Paul did a quick examination of his patient and then faced Dodge and Bryan. 'I need light — bring in every lamp you have in the place. Any mirrors will help too. Place them where they will magnify the light.'

'Is there a chance?' Dodge asked hopefully. 'Can you save them?'

Paul hated the fact he would ask such a question in front of Sarah and her husband. Rather than answer, he looked to the stove and Martha.

'Let me know as soon as the water is good and hot and don't forget about the towels.'

Kip hurried over to tend the stove and keep watch on the water. It freed up Martha for other chores.

While Dodge and Bryan scrounged two lamps and a mirror to add to the room's lighting, the midwife collected some clean towels and brought them over to the bed. She stood there like a proper nurse ready to help.

Paul supervised the placement of the lamps and mirror. Once satisfied it was the best lighting he could get, he removed a bottle of chloroform and a wad of cotton from his bag. He dampened the cotton and mustered up a positive smile for Sarah.

'This will smell sweet,' he told her soothingly. 'You only have to inhale normally and close your eyes.'

She hesitated, grimacing from anxiety and pain. 'Will I . . . ' she swallowed a sob of uncertainty, 'will I ever wake up again?'

'Not to worry, young lady,' Paul told her gently, displaying an easy confidence. 'You just relax and breathe normally. Everything is going to be just fine.'

He placed the cotton over her nose

and mouth. Within a few seconds she was no longer conscious. Once Paul felt Sarah was completely under he turned to the midwife, who had neatly arranged the linen and towels on a nearby chair.

'I'm sorry, I didn't get your name?'

'It's Martha Gundersund,' she replied.

'Martha, I need you to administer the anesthesia and stand ready to help with the towels. Will you do that?'

'Of course,' she answered, 'anything you wish.'

He showed her the procedure for keeping the cotton damp with chloroform so Sarah would not regain consciousness. Once she had taken over that chore, he tested the water and found it was adequately heated.

'Sheriff, you and the other two gents need to wait outside.'

'There's no way I'm . . . ' Bryan balked.

'One grain of dust kicked up by your shoes,' Paul informed him in a curt tone of voice, 'one minute particle of dirt from a sleeve or even a stirring of the air from your breathing and it could mean infection. Believe me when I tell you a lot more women die of infection during childbirth than from complications or internal bleeding. You will all have to wait outside.'

'Enough said.' Dodge accepted his word. 'Let's get some air, Bryan, Kip. The doc here knows what he's doing.'

'The doc?' Bryan blurted. 'But ain't he the faro dealer?'

Dodge opened the door. 'Let's go, boys.'

Paul watched the men until they headed out the door and returned to his patient. It had been a long time since he'd done any surgery. *Maybe too long!* He could sense the nightmares at the back of his mind, poised to assail his senses and attack his calm. He inhaled deeply and let the breath out slowly, striving to control his emotions. There were two lives at stake and he had to be both steady and strong.

The room was silent, the air completely still inside the house. Martha had not spoken up while the three men were present. Now she looked at Paul expectantly, holding her breath.

'You're going to take the baby.'

It was a statement so he only nodded his assent. With a grim determination, he dipped the scalpel into the hot water and sloshed it about to clean the blade. Holding it up he paused a second to study his hand. Remarkably, there was no trembling, no shaking; he was as steady as he had ever been in his life. He closed his eyes, uttered a silent prayer and started to work.

2

It was a social gathering for Seth Calloway's family. Seth and his sons, Ken and Andrew were playing cards. Andrew's two girls were pulling taffy and having a great time with Seth's grown daughter, Jenny. Both his and Andrew's wife were sewing and stitching to make a couple new outfits for the girls.

Seth glanced at his last boy living at home. Ken was a half-dozen years older than Jenny and whenever they had family get-togethers like this, he often got the itch to be married. He loved kids and the idea of having his own home, but there were twenty men for every woman in that part of Wyoming, so the pickings were pretty lean. He hadn't found himself a girl and as for Jenny, she seemed to lack a girl's usual interest or enthusiasm for matrimony.

She had refused the amorous advances of no less than a dozen men since reaching her courting years. Cute as she was — favoring her ma on that count — he feared the girl was going to end up an old spinster.

'Play's to you, Pa,' Ken said. 'That's my ace of diamonds.'

Seth cleared his throat and rejoined the card-game. 'Sorry, boys,' he excused his lack of interest, 'I was thinking about the barn dance next Saturday night.'

'You figuring to take Ma and enter the dance competition?' Andrew teased. 'I remember you telling us a thousand times how you and she used to cut and stack the straw during a square-dance.'

'Hear, hear,' Ken joined in. 'Put everyone else to shame . . . leastways, that's what you've been telling us all these years.'

Seth smiled. 'I guess the stories do tend to grow a little taller with age, and me and your ma were both a lot younger then.' He sobered. 'But no, I'm wondering if Jenny is intending to go.'

Ken uttered a cynical grunt. 'You mean like last month when we twisted her arm and forced her to come along with us?' He scowled at the memory. 'She must have turned down an offer to dance from every eligible guy within a hundred miles that night.'

'Only one I saw her dance with was the storekeeper,' Andrew agreed. 'Being that his wife is about to drop foal, Sarah couldn't dance anything but the real slow tunes.'

'Sarah married a good man,' Seth commented. 'I sometimes wonder if Jenny might have had a soft spot for Bryan, back before he asked Sarah to marry him.'

'You think maybe Jenny was in love with her best friend's beau?'

'It happens,' Seth said quietly.

'I reckon Bryan was the town catch, what with his dad leaving him the general store.'

'Jenny wouldn't have been interested in him because he had a store and a little money,' Ken declared. 'You know how she is, always trying to find a book to read and she gets that *Harper's Monthly Magazine* in the mail every few weeks. I think she's looking for an educated sort, maybe a newspaper man or traveling salesman of some kind.'

'She wouldn't settle for some wandering drummer,' Andrew argued. 'She comes from a family with roots and is going to want to put down her own roots too.'

Seth decided they had discussed his daughter long enough. He checked his cards and played a jack of clubs.

'Got to trump that there ace, Ken,' he said without apology. 'I might have warned you I was short one suit.'

Ken groaned. 'Yeah, some warning — take the only ace in my hand!'

The door to the house suddenly flew open and Lester Calloway, Seth's nephew, burst into the room. His face was flushed and tears were in his eyes. He struggled to stifle a sob as he spoke.

'Ned has been killed!' he wailed. 'It

happened not more than an hour ago.'

Seth jumped to his feet. 'Ned?' he repeated. 'Someone killed Ned?'

'Bet it was one of them dirty damn farmers!' Andrew declared.

The women came in from the other room, shocked at the news and each clamoring for more information.

Seth held up a hand and brought silence to the room. 'Are you sure about this, boy?' he asked Lester.

His nephew bobbed his head up and down. 'Jingo and Sage were in town. Soon as they heard the news they come running. They said Sheriff Roper had put the man who done it in jail.'

'If he's in jail,' Seth concluded, 'it must have been murder!'

'Them filthy land-hog squatters are gonna pay!' Andrew vowed.

'One of the farmers killed Ned?' Jenny asked Lester. 'Who did it?'

However, Lester changed his head shaking to a side-to-side movement. 'It warn't done by no farmer. Jingo said it was a shoot-out betwixt Ned and a faro dealer.'

'If it was a fair fight, why arrest the man?' Andrew wanted to know.

'To keep him alive.' Ken sneered the answer. 'Roper knows we won't stand for some pasteboard slinger killing one of our own!'

'Hiding him behind a badge ain't gonna save him,' Lester vowed. 'Pa says we're gonna ride to town first thing tomorrow. We'll sure 'nuff hang the dealer from the livery block and tackle — the one they use for loading the wagons. We'll string him up for the whole town to see.'

Seth gave Lester a nod. 'We'll be ready to ride with you fellows at first light.'

Lester displayed a new sadness. 'Can't hardly believe Ned ain't coming home again,' he said. 'Tom and me was just joking about him sneaking off by himself with his share of money from selling off them half-dozen mustangs we broke to ride this morning. We figured he would drink himself into a stupor and maybe buy one of the dance-hall gals a few drinks.' He grew somber again. 'We never thought he would get himself kilt.'

Seth used a sympathetic tone. 'Tell Buford we're all real sorry, Lester.'

Lester fought back tears as he turned for the door. 'Yeah, I'll tell him, Uncle Seth.' Then he went out into the dark and closed the door behind him.

'This sure don't look good, Pa.' Andrew was first to speak. 'If Sheriff Roper put that dealer in jail, he is going to be hell-bent on protecting him.'

'When the farmers get word about Ned they will likely take the gambler's side,' Ken added. 'Could end up facing the whole bunch of them when we show up.'

'If we ride in first thing in the morning, maybe they won't have time to get organized and come to the killer's defense!' Seth declared.

'I'd hate to have to fight against Roper,' Ken admitted. 'He always seemed a decent sort.'

'Yeah,' Andrew agreed, 'And we all

went hunting and fishing with Bryan over near the Dakotas last summer. He won't be happy to have us going up against his dad-in-law.'

Seth held up a hand to stop any further discussion. 'We don't brand the calf until he is roped and pinned. We'll ride in with Buford and his boys and see what the day brings.'

'I'm going too.' Jenny spoke up.

'You stay at home, squirt!' Andrew spoke up.

'Might be gun play.' Ken joined in with his brother. 'You're the only Calloway girl still living at home. Wouldn't do to have you get in the path of a bullet.'

'You were talking about Bryan getting involved, Andrew,' she retorted. 'Sarah has been my best friend since we settled here and she is due to have her baby any day now. I won't get in the middle of your fight, but I want to be there. I'll visit with Sarah while you men sort out the trouble, but I'm going too.'

'It's her dad we might be going up against,' Ken argued. 'She might not feel like socializing with a Calloway, friend or no.'

'Sarah knows I won't take sides against her family!'

She and her two brothers looked expectantly at Seth. He made all of the family decisions . . . with occasional input from Mrs Calloway. Mother Calloway chose this moment to speak.

'Sarah was carrying the baby real low when we saw her at the last Sunday meeting,' she said quietly. 'Be my guess, the baby might already be here.'

'All right, you can come along,' Seth told Jenny, 'but you stay shed of any trouble. I'll not be losing a son or daughter to a stray bullet.'

'I'll visit with Sarah,' Jenny promised. 'That's all I'll do.'

'Too bad about Ned.' Andrew returned to the original subject. 'He was something of a bully and could be a real pain in the neck sometimes, but he was kin.'

Ken nodded his agreement. 'I won't

31

miss the way he always liked to push me around, but I never wished him dead.'

'If a man draws a gun on another man with malice in his heart, the odds are one or both of them is going to die,' Seth observed. 'Sounds as if Ned picked the wrong man to tangle with.'

Ken gathered the cards and put the deck away. The time for playing games was over.

'Guess we'll call it a night,' Andrew said, rising up from the table. 'It's past the kid's bedtime and it sounds like we'll need an early start. I'll be here before sun-up.'

'Let's hope this don't spill over into a war with the town folks,' Ken displayed a grave expression. 'If Sheriff Roper refuses to allow Uncle Buford to get justice with that there dealer, we could wind up facing the whole town.'

'That's the truth,' Andrew agreed, 'and we already have our hands full with those encroaching farmers. If the town folk take sides against us, we won't have a friend in the whole valley.'

Seth got his goodbye hugs from his grandchildren and watched them leave with Andrew and his wife. He felt a pang of uncertainty. They had worked so long and hard to build up the two ranches. What if Ned's death started an all-out war?

He sighed and kept the worry to himself. 'Let's get to bed,' he told the members of his family. 'It's likely to be a long day tomorrow.'

★　★　★

Paul took a last look at his handiwork and stepped away from the bed. He placed his hands on his hips and arched his back, stiff from bending over Sarah.

'That it?' Martha asked, prepared to remove the cotton wad from Sarah's mouth and nose.

Paul gave her a nod, so she put down the cotton and returned the cap to the bottle of chloroform. She placed it next to his medical bag, then walked over and stood right in front of him. Without a word of warning, she rose up on her toes and kissed Paul on the cheek.

'Never in all my born days have I witnessed anything as miraculous as what you did,' she said tenderly. Stepping back, she added: 'God surely smiled down on Sarah this night, having you here.'

'It's a relatively simple procedure,' he replied, embarrassed by both her action and her praise. 'Infection is our main concern now. I used some carbolic acid for antiseptic, but it's still wait and see for a few days.'

Martha took a few moments to clean the healthy baby girl and wrap her in a blanket. During that time, Paul carefully secured a bandage to cover the stitches across Sarah's abdomen. The patient began to stir by the time he had finished. Paul spoke to her in a soothing voice and spoon-fed her a sip of laudanum to help ease her pain. He warned her that she would feel the effects of the caesarean delivery and be sore for several days to come.

Sarah shrugged off her drowsiness and searched the room for her child. Martha hurried over to lay the baby in her arms, careful to avoid placing the child too low, where she might press against the freshly sutured area.

Paul went to the door and opened it. The anxiety on the faces of Bryan and Dodge gave proof of the strain of their waiting and worrying. Kip had left, probably because he felt this was a personal event for the family. Whether it turned out good or bad, the two men most affected would have each other for consolation or joy.

'You can come in,' Paul told them. 'The baby seems fine.'

'My wife?' Bryan asked at once.

'She is doing fine too for the present. We'll have to keep a close eye until she heals.'

Bryan reached out and grabbed Paul's hand. He pumped it until Paul felt his fingers grow numb.

'I can't thank you enough!' The man

gushed forth his gratitude. 'What you did! It's . . . it's the greatest thing to ever happen in my life! I mean it! You saved my baby and my wife!'

'Your wife still has to mend without infection,' Paul warned him.

Bryan didn't seem to hear. He released the grip on Paul's hand and rushed over to be with his wife.

'You're a mystery, Warrick,' the sheriff declared. 'Ready to forfeit your life one minute and saving a woman and child the next.'

'I haven't saved your daughter yet, Sheriff. With any surgery there's a chance of complications. If she doesn't develop any medical problems within a few days, we can all breathe a little easier.'

Dodge went over to admire his grandchild while Paul used the last of the hot water to clean his instruments and put his medical supplies back in the valise. Martha took on the chore of returning the lamps and mirrors to their usual places and collected the bloody towels for laundering. Each time Paul looked her direction she would smile. He wondered if the matronly lady would tell her husband that she had kissed a strange man this night.

After a few minutes Dodge placed his hand on his daughter's head and told her he loved her. With a last glance at his new granddaughter, he moved over to stand next to Paul.

'After what you did here, Warrick, there ain't no way I'm going to let the Calloways put a noose around your neck.'

'I don't want anyone getting killed on my account, Sheriff.'

Dodge snorted. 'I'm a suck-egg mule if you ain't the most peculiar man I ever met, Warrick! You just saved my daughter and her baby. What kind of man would I be if I handed you over to the Calloway bunch?'

'A live one.'

'Buford is going to have to allow that his boy got himself killed in a fair fight. That's all there is to it.'

'Of course, I've heard of what a forgiving man Buford can be. I'm sure he'll accept your word as law.'

'I'm the sheriff. My word *is* law!'

'I told you before, my life isn't worth anyone getting hurt or killed. If the Calloways come after me, let me deal with them on my own.'

'*On your own* meaning they will kill you!'

'You want me in a cell or can I sleep in my own bed tonight?' Paul asked, dropping the subject.

Dodge heaved a sigh. 'Sleep wherever you want.' He added quickly, 'But report in to me first thing in the morning. We'll decide what to do then.'

Paul took his bag and turned for the door. Before making his exit he stopped. 'Tell Sarah not to move around or try to sit up straight tonight. I don't want any undue pressure on her stitches.'

'I'll tell her.'

'If I'm still alive come morning, I'll be round to check on her and change the dressing.'

'Thank you for what you did here tonight, Warrick,' the sheriff said quietly, a sincere reverence in his voice, 'I mean that with all my heart.'

Paul didn't reply but headed for the darkness. A lamp from a house or two gave off enough light for him to see his way. He walked over to the main street and turned toward the boarding-house at the edge of town. It was a pleasant evening, not too warm and not too cool. It was rare to have not the slightest stir of breeze, as Wyoming had its share of wind . . . more than a normal share, actually. Paul thought back over the past three years. He had wandered to many places seeking to put his nightmares to rest.

Well, bucko, he mused, *the Calloway family just might fix your memory and sleeping problems . . . permanently!*

3

Paul had enjoyed a dreamless sleep during the night. It was a relief to not awaken several times in a cold sweat, haunted by visions of blood, wretchedness and devastation. It was doubly odd considering he had killed a man the previous night, the first man he had ever been forced to shoot. Logically, he attributed the peaceful slumber to the fact he had done something good for the first time since the war. He had actually saved the lives of a woman and her child.

Or so he hoped! he warned himself. There was still a chance of infection. He could not count Sarah as a success until she had fully mended from the operation.

Paul reported to the sheriff at sun-up. Rather than confine Paul in a jail cell, Dodge allowed he was free to move around. He warned him to stay out of sight, insistent upon talking to Buford on his own and trying to head off a confrontation over Ned's death.

Paul was finishing breakfast at the eatery when a dozen riders entered town. He had never met Buford Calloway, but most of the ranchers and hired hands had the same look about them. Heavy denim jeans, thick woolen shirts, sporting leather vests or durable jackets, some wearing chaps, each with a Western style hat and riding-boots. Most every rider had a length of rope coiled at the saddle, secured by a rawhide strap, and a poncho or bedroll was tightly cinched behind the heavy cowpuncher saddle. They were all heavily armed — pistol at the hip and rifle in hand or tucked in a riding-boot — grim-faced, with weather-hardened features and the cold, flinty eyes of men on a deadly mission. All except one.

Upon closer inspection he discovered there was an unarmed girl among them. She broke away from the others before they reached the saloon and rode over to the livery instead.

Paul pushed aside the plate from what might be his last meal. It wouldn't do for the Calloway bunch to hang him before he had a final visit with Sarah. He wanted to ensure the new infant was doing well and to instruct the young mother on the care needed to prevent infection to her incision. Martha could remove the stitches when the time came.

He took a few minutes to finish his coffee and then paid for the meal. The café owner allowed Paul to leave by the rear door so he would not be seen from the street. Once outside he took the long way around to reach Bryan and Sarah's house. He knocked and listened for Sarah to invite him inside, before he opened the door. He figured Bryan would be at work but discovered his patient was not alone. The guest was the same girl he had seen ride in with the Calloway bunch not five minutes earlier!

'I can come back,' he offered, standing framed in the doorway.

'No, no,' Sarah said quickly. 'This is Jenny Calloway, my dearest friend.'

'Calloway?' He repeated the name. 'You are related to Ned Calloway?'

The young woman gave a slight nod of her head. 'He was my cousin.'

Paul gave her a sympathetic nod and appraised her momentarily. There was no ring on her finger although she was probably in her mid to late twenties. She wore a dark riding-skirt, snug jacket over a calico-colored blouse, with riding-boots and a woman's Western style hat tipped slightly to one side on her head. Her features were petite, a finely sculptured jaw, slightly upturned nose, with sensuous lips and bright, shimmering green eyes. The goldenrod-colored hair had been pulled back into a ponytail, but a bang spilled forth to decorate her brow. She was pert, vibrant and far and away the best-looking Calloway he had ever seen.

'I'm very sorry about Ned,' Paul told

her softly. 'I mean that.'

She sobered appropriately before asking: 'You're a real doctor?'

'I used to be a surgeon,' he evaded, 'but I haven't practiced medicine for some time.'

'Come in and shut the door,' Sarah spoke up. 'I was just showing Jenny what a beautiful girl you helped bring into the world.'

'She's a special baby,' Paul agreed, enjoying the way Sarah beamed. 'How did she do last night?'

'Only cried once,' Sarah replied. Then she laughed. 'Of course, Bryan hardly put her down for most of the night, not until he had to go open the store this morning. I think she's going to be spoiled rotten.'

'Kids need to be spoiled on occasion,' Paul said, stepping over to the bed so he could study the mother and child.

Sarah had the baby cuddled in the crook of her arm. Paul was relieved to note the healthy flush of color of both patients. Their cheeks were bathed in a soft pink glow and Sarah's eyes were bright, while the baby had her eyes open, but was too young to focus on specific people or objects yet.

Paul turned to the attractive visitor. 'Miss Calloway, I wonder if you would mind taking the baby outside while I check Sarah's stitches and change her bandage?'

'Certainly,' Jenny agreed.

Paul slipped one hand under the baby's body and his other beneath her head. He lifted the infant and carefully placed her in Jenny's waiting arms.

'You said outside?' Jenny asked, perplexed by the request.

'To safeguard from infection,' he told her. 'It only takes a tiny bit of dust to contaminate an injury.'

'It's the doctor's rules,' Sarah said lightly. 'Take Paulette outside. It'll only take a minute or two.'

Paul was stunned at hearing the baby's name. 'Paulette?'

Sarah smiled. 'Yes, Bryan and I

agreed we should name her after the man who saved both of our lives.' With a twinkle of humor, 'And Paulette sounded better than *Warrick* for a first name, especially for a girl.'

'I don't know what to say,' Paul said, immediately humbled. 'I'm greatly honored.'

'Come on, Paulette.' Jenny whispered the words to the baby. 'Let's you and me go out on the front porch and I'll introduce you to the great big world of the outdoors.'

Once the pair had made their exit and closed the door, Paul used the utmost care to inspect and remove the bandage. Even with his being careful, Sarah sucked in her breath a time or two from the tenderness.

'Did you take any laudanum last night?' he asked, while checking for any sign of infection.

'No.'

'That's good, as long as you didn't need it. But I left it for you in case you began to suffer too much pain.'

Sarah regarded him with a serious look. 'I once had a friend who had terrible headaches. She started taking laudanum and got to the point where she was having a sip or two every hour. She finally got to the point where she couldn't function without downing a dose of laudanum first. The last time I saw her, she wandered about as if lost in a thick fog. She got killed when she walked in front of a fast-moving stagecoach. I don't want that to happen to me.'

'We discovered after the war that a good many men had become overly reliant on drugs,' Paul agreed. 'However, a sip or two can also help a person get through a painful episode.'

'Jenny told me Ned was killed in a gunfight last night.' Sarah changed the subject.

'Yes, I was there.'

'I guess he was hurt too bad for you to help, huh?'

'Dead when he hit the floor,' Paul replied truthfully.

'Never cared for him much,' Sarah said, watching as Paul began to affix a new bandage over her stitches. 'He sometimes came in the store when I was helping out.' She uttered a girlish giggle, 'Before I got too big to get down the aisles, that is. Anyway, he had a way of looking at me just so, like I was a beef critter and he was real hungry. You know what I mean?'

'I fear most men have looked upon a woman in such a fashion,' Paul admitted. 'The difficulty for us men is to hide our yearning to maul a beautiful woman and instead pretend to be a gentleman.'

She started to laugh and stopped herself. 'Oh, not fair making me laugh until I can really let loose. Right now it hurts too much.'

He gave her a smile. 'Fair enough.'

'How am I doing?' she asked.

'There was a small amount of bleeding but there's no sign of infection. We'll hope it stays that way. If I'm around tomorrow. I'll stop by and change the bandage one more time.'

'You going some place?'

'I don't know, Sarah. It's not really up to me.'

She frowned at his odd remark while he pulled her gown back into place and backed up a step.

'If I'm not able to come by, have Martha change the dressing for you. The stitches can come out in two weeks.'

Still looking puzzled at his comment she said she would follow his orders.

'I'll tell Jenny you are ready for visitors.' He pivoted about, started for the door, but paused to speak over his shoulder. 'Just be careful about any sudden movement until those stitches have time to heal.'

'Doctor?' Sarah stopped him with the still unfamiliar title. When he paused to look back at her, she displayed a heartfelt sincerity. 'I . . . *we* can never thank you enough for what you've done. You were a godsent blessing for me and Paulette.'

Paul felt a rush of emotion block off his vocal cords and a distinct trickle of warmth entered his being. He had been dead inside for so long. Her endearing gratitude was a thread of sunshine slicing through a heavy shroud of gloom. If not for the fact that he was going to die today, he might have felt there was some hope for the future.

Opening the door, he discovered Jenny playfully cooing at the baby. She showed him an innocent and honest smile.

'She's beautiful,' she murmured, lifting Paulette up to where she could kiss her on the cheek. 'Nothing in the world is as lovely as a newborn child.'

Paul regained the use of his voice. 'Uttered like the words of a future mother,' he said. 'I'm sure one day you will have your own child to fuss over.'

Jenny laughed. 'If I ever find the right man. I swear I must be the hardest person in the country to please.'

'An eye-catching lady such as your-self?' His brows pinched closer in disbelief. 'I would think you would have more suitors than a person could count.'

Jenny accepted the flattery gracefully but grew serious. 'There are suitors aplenty, but I'm not of a mind to marry a wrangler or cowpuncher.'

'Oh? What kind of man are you looking for?'

Her eyes lit up and a flush of enthusiasm instilled a girlish lilt in her voice. 'I want a man who is educated; a man who can tell me stories about faraway places. He should be charming and kind and gentle and loving. He will enjoy having me dress in my finest gown to take me out to a fancy dining place and then to a theater for a play or opera. I want to travel, see more of the world than the next pasture or expanse of desert.' She sighed, as if the idea was impossible. 'Is that so wrong?'

'Not at all.'

'You being a doctor and all, you must have seen a lot of territory,' she deduced. 'I'll bet you've been to big cities too. Have you ridden on one of them new fancy Pullman train cars, or maybe a luxurious hansom cab?'

He smiled at the sparkle of fervor in her eyes and zeal in her voice.

'I believe hansom cabs are used primarily in England,' he said, 'but I did ride an omnibus back in New York a few times. There's nothing very glamorous about one of those.'

'Yeah, but you know what I mean,' she persisted. 'There's nothing out here but wind, dust and cows. I know I'll probably end up living here, but I want to visit a big city, see something of the rest of the world first.'

'And maybe take a promenade down Broadway to see the opera?'

A bright smile lit up her face. It reminded Paul of a child on Christmas morning.

'Yes, that's it exactly.'

'I expect you would make a fine lady, Miss Calloway,' he told her seriously. 'I can picture you decked out in an evening gown, with a velvet wrap about your shoulders, parading down a cobble-stone avenue to one of the grand theaters. I should think you would be the belle of New York or any other big city.'

Instead of adding to her eagerness his words kindled a grim resolve. She lowered her head as if in defeat. 'It's only a faraway dream,' she murmured. 'I'm sure to end up living in a dirt-floor cabin with a house full of kids, waiting for my husband to get home from fifteen hours in the saddle. The furthermost east I'll ever get will probably be Cheyenne to buy or sell cattle.'

'I believe they have a nice theater in Denver,' he offered. 'That wouldn't be too far to travel one day.'

But the eagerness had disappeared and her expression was resolved, even despondent. 'Yes, maybe,' she agreed, matter-of-factly.

Paul decided it was time to face his own future . . . or lack thereof. He said: 'I wish you good luck with your dreams, Miss Calloway. I hope you find what you're looking for.'

Jenny offered him the semblance of a smile and entered the house. Once she and the baby were safely inside, Paul turned and walked up the street. He would find a place to sit down and wait. Dodge had instructed him not to come round until the Calloway bunch had left town, so he would put off his visit to jail until later. He hoped no one started a fight. He didn't want any more crippled or dead men on his conscience. If the cattlemen demanded his death, he would make it easy for them.

★   ★   ★

The veins in Buford's face stood out as if ready to explode. Facing Sheriff Roper, Bryan and Kip Hadley, he and his two boys, Tom and Lester, were ready to fight. Only Seth held his brother and sons back, using a restraining hand and a firm tone of voice.

'Let's listen to what Roper has to say, Buford,' he told his brother. 'The man has been our friend for a good many years.'

Buford was not ready to be appeased. 'Friend or foe, it don't matter none! Ned was gunned down and his killer is going to pay!'

Seth tipped his head at the sheriff. 'Speak your piece, Roper,' he said. 'Best be quick about it.'

'Yeah,' Lester snarled the words, 'you can talk till you turn blue in the face, but it ain't gonna' change nuthin'. We're gonna hang the man who done kilt our brother!'

'First of all, Seth, Buford,' Dodge explained carefully, 'it was Ned who pushed the faro dealer into the fight. He's the one who wouldn't back off.'

'Probably got tired of getting cheated!' Tom bellowed.

'Yeah!' Lester joined in. 'Everyone knows them games are crooked!'

'He shouldn't have been playing in the first place,' Dodge maintained, keeping his voice even and under control. 'He was drunk, surly and spoiling for a fight. His mistake was choosing the wrong man to push.'

'Get on to telling us the name of the murdering jasper!' Buford roared. 'Who kilt my boy?'

'In the second place,' Dodge continued as if he hadn't heard the man, 'Ned pulled iron first. Every man jack in the saloon witnessed it. The dealer had to shoot or Ned would have gunned him down in cold blood.'

'That's the God's truth!' Kip avowed. 'If he'd been the one to live, he would be facing a hangman's noose for murder.'

Buford glared at both the sheriff and his sometimes deputy. 'I still ain't heard nuthen what will save that polecat from getting his neck stretched.'

'I'm telling you, if you'll shut up and let me finish,' Dodge growled the words, momentarily losing his composure.

'So talk already!' Lester shouted.

'Ain't no one stopping you!'

Dodge knew he could not reason with Buford, so he directed his argument at Seth. 'Turns out the faro dealer used to be a doctor, a surgeon,' he said, gravely serious and in control again. 'Last night, my girl had complications with the delivery of her baby. She and the unborn child were both about to die in childbirth. That faro dealer was the one who saved the life of both my daughter and new grandbaby!'

'Why'n tarnation would a doctor be dealing faro?' Seth asked cynically. 'You can't tell me there ain't no sick people around to tend to!'

'I don't know that part of the story,' Dodge admitted, 'but I swear to you all, my girl and her baby would both have died without his help. The midwife will tell you as much too.'

'Just tell us where he is!' Buford continued his quest for vengeance. 'I don't give a tinker's damn for whatever else the man has done, he's got a rendezvous with a length of hemp!'

Seth, however, had listened to the sheriff's story. He glanced at Andrew and then at Tom, Buford's oldest boy. Tom had a wife and three kids of his own. Every husband understood the danger involved in childbirth. Thousands of women died each year from infection, bleeding or complications. The news gave each of them cause to pause and consider what Dodge had told them.

The sheriff took advantage of their hesitancy and continued to plead his case. 'The man didn't want to kill Buford's boy, Seth. Ned didn't give him any choice; he forced him to shoot. Ned drew down on the doctor with murder in his heart and forced the man to defend himself.'

'No one kills a Calloway and gets away with it!' Lester shouted, still as wound up as Buford. 'You tell us where he is or we'll tear this town apart!'

With a firm set of his jaw, Dodge now pointed the double-barrel, twelve-gauge shotgun at Lester.

'Trust me when I say I'm not going to stand by while you kill the man who saved my daughter and her child. If it means a fight, I'll sure enough bring twin loads of buckshot to the party.'

'What about you, Bryan?' Seth asked, before his brother could take up the gauntlet. 'Do you also say the man saved your girl and wife?'

'Sarah couldn't deliver — the baby was ready but couldn't come. Martha Gunderson was there to help — the same as she has helped to bring dozens of children in to this world here in Liberty. She flat out told me both of them were going to die.' He stood shoulder to shoulder with Dodge and stared squarely at Seth. 'I was there; I seen it! My girl and unborn child were both dying right before my eyes. I sent Kip to fetch Dodge so he could say goodbye. That's when the faro dealer told Dodge he used to be a doctor.'

'It's all true,' Kip was the one to speak next. 'The sheriff and the doc rushed over to Bryan's house, whilst I ran and got his medical bag from his room. When I got there with his valise, the doc starts giving all of us orders. Afore you know it, me, the sheriff and Bryan are shoved out to the front porch, while he cuts Sarah open and takes the baby. He saved both of their lives, he sure 'nuff did. It was a miracle him being able to do that.'

Buford was still snorting and huffing like a bull ready to charge. But the story had penetrated Seth's rage. The blood-lust drained from his face.

'Where is he?' Buford demanded to know. 'You best tell us right now, Roper!'

Seth took a step back and laid a hand on his brother's shoulder. 'You know how Ned was when he drank, Buford,' he said gently. 'Your boy could sometimes be meaner than a scalded badger.'

Buford's eyes grew wide and a sneer curled his lips. 'You ain't gonna blame this on Ned! He's the one who ended up dead! Some faro-dealing buck kilt him and I aim to have my pound of flesh!'

'You heard what these men told us, the man saved a woman and her child! What kind of man shoots a fellow dead one minute, then does a good deed like that the next?'

'It don't make no never mind to me! He's got to pay the full price for my boy's life!'

'Pa's right!' Lester affirmed. 'An eye for an eye!'

A small army of men approached from along the walk attracting the attention of both parties. Mort Gastone led the group — three of whom worked at the casino, along with the town's tinsmith, his son-in-law and two other businessmen from town. Their faces were grave and they were all packing iron.

'You'll not be hanging an innocent man here today, Buford.' Mort spoke up. 'Your son started the fight with my dealer. He drew his gun and was going to kill him. If I had been quick enough,

I would have shot Ned in the back to save my dealer's life.'

'It was a fair fight,' spoke up another of the group. 'I was there and seen it too. Ned was sure enough going to smoke that dealer, whether he had a gun or not.'

The men lined up next to the sheriff, ready to fight if it became necessary.

'You don't scare us,' Buford sounded off. 'If we have to walk over a dozen men to get to my boy's murderer, that's what we'll do!'

'Easy now, boys!' Dodge said in a tranquil voice, cradling his shotgun in his right hand, while raising his left hand to calm them all down. 'We don't want to start a war on the main street of Liberty. Killing each other won't change the facts or bring Ned back to life.'

He lowered his hand enough to point a finger at Buford. 'You've no call for starting a fight over this, Buford. No crime was committed. Your boy started a fight and lost. He was killed in an act of self-defense.'

'Any one of us would have done the same,' Mort agreed. 'Ned didn't leave my dealer any choice.'

'And he saved the life of my wife and baby!' Bryan spoke up. 'There's no way I can stand back and let you kill him, not for defending himself.'

Buford reached for his gun. Dodge leveled the shotgun.

But Seth quickly grabbed hold of his brother's wrist, pinning his hand to the butt of his pistol.

'No, Buford!' he told him sternly. 'There is no fight here. It won't serve Ned's memory any good by throwing lead at these men and getting a lot of us killed too.'

Buford glared at Seth, his teeth bared in a snarl, spoiling for a fight. He raised his free hand as if he would push Seth away. However, he stopped in mid-motion while his brain worked hard to pump the coolness of reason into his hot-tempered rage. To pull his gun was to die. Dodge was not bluffing.

Seth refused to give ground and

Buford had never been able to dominate his elder brother. Seth was the one with reason, the leader of the Calloway clan, the man who made the smart choices. Buford knew it; and more than that, he had always respected his brother's decisions. Slowly, the wrath subsided. It melted away, leaving behind the deep and agonizing pain of losing a son.

'He was my eldest boy,' Buford said thickly, holding back a sob of grief. 'He was my foreman, the man who would have one day taken over my ranch.'

'It weren't meant to be,' Seth told him soothingly. 'The boy was too wild, too anxious to use his fists or a gun. We can't let our sorrow rule our thinking, Buford. You pull that hog-leg here and you'll maybe get yourself and your other two sons killed too. What's done is over; it's too late to change anything now. You have to accept what has happened and continue on. It's all you can do.'

Buford lowered his head to hide the

tears in his eyes. 'I . . . I 'spect you're right, Seth,' he conceded at last. 'Killing a dozen men wouldn't settle the score. Nothing is going to bring my boy back.'

Seth patted his brother on the back and put a hard stare on the sheriff. 'It would be best all around if Ned's killer left town. A tragedy like this can sure enough fester until it comes to a head. If you want that man to stay healthy, he had best leave this part of the country and never come back.'

Dodge Roper gave a nod of agreement. 'Kip will help you with your boy,' he said, glancing over at his deputy. 'And once more, let me say how we're all real sorry for your loss.'

'I've got Ned laid out in a box over at the ice-house,' Kip told the Calloway bunch. 'You're welcome to borrow my wagon to take him home, if that's where you want to bury him.'

'We'll put him in the family cemetery, next to Uncle Josh,' Seth replied. 'Come on, Buford, let's get your boy and take him home.'

4

Jenny left Sarah and went looking for her father and brothers. She reached the general store before she spied Ken up at the far end of town. He was at the livery, securing Ned's horse with a lead rope. She paused to look around but Buford, her father and the others were nowhere to be seen.

Ken was busy with the horses and didn't notice her until Jenny approached to within a few steps. He turned his head, saw it was her, and returned to the chore at hand.

'Where is everybody?' Jenny asked.

'They took Ned home for burial,' Ken replied, working to secure the rope to a tie-ring on the back of his saddle. 'We're about fifteen minutes behind them.'

Jenny scanned the street a second time. 'I don't see a body swinging from a rope and I didn't hear any gunfire. Did Ned's killer leave town?'

Ken cleared his throat as if embarrassed. 'We talked it over with Sheriff Roper and decided the guy was only defending himself.'

Jenny did not conceal her surprise. 'Buford went along with that?'

'Pa had to talk sense to him for a spell,' Ken admitted. 'And I can tell you things were right tense for a bit. I was about as nervous as a three-legged cat surrounded by a pack of bloodthirsty hounds.' He tossed a glance over his shoulder at Jenny. She didn't speak, waiting for him to continue.

'Roper was joined by more than a half-dozen men from town,' Ken explained. 'They were all armed and ready to fight. If Pa hadn't been able to calm Buford down, I figure there would have been bodies all over the street.' He let out a sigh, as if he had been holding his breath for a long period of time. 'I got to tell you, Sis, my heart was pounding like a war drum. I thought we were all about to die.'

Jenny shook her head back and forth in amazement. 'Where did Ned's killer find so many loyal friends? I never dreamed the men around town would stand up to Pa and Buford, not with you and the others there too.'

'Actually, it was your girlfriend's husband who tipped the scales.'

'Bryan?'

'He claimed the faro dealer had saved Sarah and his baby's life.' Ken shrugged his shoulders. 'Guess he must have been a medic or something at one time.'

The news hit Jenny like a wet branch across her face. 'The doctor!' she gasped. 'He killed Cousin Ned?'

Her reaction caused Ken to regard her with a curious look. 'That's what we were told,' he explained. 'Sheriff Roper stood before us, shotgun in hand and said he would die before letting us have the man who had saved his daughter and her child. Bryan was right at his side, along with Mort Gaston and several other men from town. I'm telling you, Sis, we were about one whisker away from being in the middle of the biggest gunfight Wyoming has ever seen.'

'Paul Warrick killed Ned,' Jenny murmured incredulously. 'I can't believe it. He seemed so polite and caring, so . . . so nice.'

Ken gave her a curious look. 'Are you telling me that you met this — you say his name is Paul Warrick?'

'He came by to tend to Sarah while I was visiting. He had me hold the baby while he changed the dressing on Sarah's stitches.' Jenny ducked her head, hating to admit the rest. 'He even stopped to speak to me when he left. He said he was very sorry about Ned.' She hissed the next words, 'But he didn't say one blasted word about being the one who did the shooting!'

'The man is a dealer in Gastone's casino one minute and the next he's a surgeon. Doesn't that strike you as pretty strange, Sis?'

'Everything about this is crazy!'

'You say the man said he was sorry about Ned?'

'Yes, very heartfelt.' Jenny sighed. 'I had no idea his remorse was due to him being the man who had killed Cousin Ned!'

'To his credit, it sounds as if Ned didn't leave him any choice. Everyone who saw it claims he had to shoot or be gunned down in cold blood.'

'Ned always was a hothead,' Jenny agreed. 'I'm surprised he lived this long.'

Ken kept silent for a moment. When he spoke again, a spark of mischief appeared in his eyes.

'So the doctor fellow, you thought he was a nice guy, huh?'

'Yes,' she answered candidly. 'He seemed very gentle and soft-spoken. I can't imagine him using a gun to kill another human being.'

'Sounds as if he really was sorry about Ned.'

'That was my impression,' she answered.

Then with anger again inflecting her voice, 'Now I know why.'

'I wonder if maybe he kept the truth from you for a reason,' Ken voiced in a teasing tone.

'What do you mean?'

Ken showed a good-natured smile. 'Look at it from his point of view, Jen. Confessing to a gal that you killed her cousin would certainly dampen any notion of romance.'

Jenny glared at her brother. 'He didn't show me any notion of romance, Kenneth Franklin Calloway!'

'No?'

'Absolutely Not!'

'My mistake.' Ken snickered. 'It sounded as if . . . ' he ended in mid-sentence, before continuing: 'Maybe I got it wrong about the man. I thought he might be a handsome sort, but now I'm guessing he's more of a crotchety old man. Probably looks like a wandering saddlebum.' Ken could not suppress a grin. 'Most likely resembles the south end of a northbound sow — that how it is?'

Jenny had grown up being teased endlessly. Her two elder sisters had been nearly grown when she came along. Her mother enjoyed telling her she was the 'pleasant surprise of her late child-bearing years'. Out of seven children, two had not reached their second birthday, mostly due to short rations and the bitter cold winters of Wyoming. Ken was already six when Jenny came into the world, with Andrew two years ahead of him. By the time Jenny started to learn her numbers and letters, both of her sisters were married and gone. That left two elder brothers to torment her all of her childhood years, and they seemed to genuinely enjoy the sport. It wasn't until her late teenage years that she had begun to fight back. Older and wiser with the passing of time, she could now hold her own and occasionally would win a battle.

'Well?' Ken continued the badgering. 'Is the man who killed Ned as old as sin and homely as a cross-eyed mule or do you maybe have a hankering for him?'

'He isn't all that old, nor is he hard to look at,' she eventually admitted, 'but I've yet to meet the man I have a *hankering* for.'

Ken gave a nod of approval. 'That's good. Not that me and the rest of the family wouldn't like to have you show an interest in a man — what with you being older than both of our sisters when they got hitched.'

'I'm the same age as Andrew's new wife and two years younger than Tom's!' Jenny defended herself.

'Yeah, but Tom has three kids already,' Ken pointed out. 'You start out too late and you'll need to have kids by the litter to catch up.'

'Look who's talking! You're the one who has begun to look and act like an old man. You best find yourself a woman before we have to send for one of those marriage-hungry girls back East and hope she is half-blind to boot!'

He chuckled at her spunky retort. 'Well, I'm just saying it wouldn't do for you to get all dreamy-eyed and bent out of sorts over the doctor. I don't 'spect he'll be living a very long life.'

'You said Buford and the others left town without putting up a fight.'

'That's what I said all right, Sis, but there's nothing to keep Uncle Buford or one of the boys from seeking out the faro dealer at a later date. If he knows what's good for him, that feller will set fire to his horse's tail and not look back until Liberty is nothing but a faraway memory.'

Jenny nodded her head in agreement, although she suffered a momentary twinge of disappointment. She didn't know what exactly defined a 'hankering', but she had certainly felt something for the doctor. With a sigh, she decided there was no need brooding on the notion. She would never have the chance to get to know Paul Warrick.

*　*　*

The three farmers were the leaders of the dozen families who had settled to work the land along Coyote Creek. There had been an impromptu meeting called at Ernest Ingersol's barn, with Milo Jackson and Hal Barlow in attendance.

'You hear about Ned Calloway being killed?' Ernie asked the two men.

'Some faro dealer shot him dead.' Jackson spoke up. 'I expected to hear how they had hung the slippery son and spat on his dead corpse by this time.'

'Me too,' Barlow joined in.

'My boy was in town and learned about it this morning. When the Calloway bunch showed up, the sheriff and a bunch of the townsfolk took up for him.' Ernie looked at each man meaningfully. 'Stood their ground with guns at the ready and told the Calloways to let him be.'

The other two men exchanged incredulous glances. 'Dodge Roper took on the Calloway clan?'

Ernie's son, Vince, had heard the story about Warrick being a doctor and how he had saved the sheriff's daughter and baby. He had come home and told Ernie about the encounter. Ernie took a moment to explain the details to the other two men.

'Don't that beat all,' Jackson said, once he had finished. 'Maybe them Calloways don't own the whole of Wyoming after all.'

'We've been searching for a way to set the odds to evens against them.' Ernie hurried on, filled with a renewed enthusiasm and a sense of optimism for the future. 'They've run roughshod over us ever since we first put plow to soil. Now is our time to act.'

'One less Calloway don't exactly tip the scales to our favor,' Barlow countered. 'With their hired hands they still have us outnumbered three to one.'

'And we've got every acre under the plow that will produce a crop, Ernie,' Jackson added. 'It isn't as if we're going to get another rush of settlers in this valley, there's simply no more room. It's nothing but hills and high-range pastures for miles in any direction. A man couldn't grow a decent crop of weeds if he was to try and start a farm up in those foothills.'

'Up till now we didn't know the town folk would ever stand up to the ranch barons, fellows. We figured the two Calloway brothers and their broods owned this valley and every man jack among them.'

'This here incident sounds like a one-time thing, Ernie. The faro dealer is a doctor and he saved the life of the sheriff's kid. It don't mean he and all them other folks are suddenly on our side.'

Ernie glowered at Milo. 'It does mean they have the backbone to stand against the Calloway clan.'

'Only if they figure they have reason to do so,' Milo maintained. 'I don't see how anything has changed.'

'Look, guys,' Ernie said eagerly, 'you're missing the bigger picture here. The fact them people in town stood against the Calloways and backed them down is huge. It means we only have to work things so they back us too.'

'If you're still thinking about bringing in fencing and blocking access to the creek, you might as well be spitting against the wind,' Milo declared. 'Neither the sheriff nor any of the people in town will back us if we try something like that.'

'Aren't you fed up with cattle grazing in your fields of corn?' Ernie cried. 'Don't you get sick and tired of having those mangy animals traipsing through your newly planted fields to get to the creek?'

'Of course,' Milo snarled back, 'but the cattle were here first. We can't cut off their water.'

'And we won't!' Ernie shot back. 'We'll fence in our fields and leave a pathway between each farm that allows access to the creek.'

Milo scoffed at the idea. 'Them cattle will sure enough knock down our fences. You can't keep them out with a couple little strands of wire.'

Ernie showed a sly grin. 'We can if we use barbed wire.'

'Barbed wire?' Barlow interjected, showing a frown. 'What'n thunder is barbed wire?'

Ernie walked over to his workbench and removed a short piece of braided wire. Every couple of inches a small coil of wire was woven into the main strand, a tough little twist with jagged ends. He held it out for the other two men to inspect.

'Damn!' Barlow said, as a tip of wire pricked his finger and brought blood to the surface. 'Those points are about as sharp as my skinning-knife!'

'My cousin sent this to me,' Ernie told the two men. 'He was at a demonstration where this kind of wire was used to fence in several head of wild maverick cattle. Them longhorns tested the wire several times and came back with blood on their snoots. Didn't take long for them to figure pushing up against this kind of wire was not a good idea.'

'It would also scratch up a horse and rider or even one of our kids.'

'Not if they know to stay shed of this devil's rope.'

'That's a name to fit the stuff. It sure looked wicked enough to have been spun by the devil.'

'This is the time to act, my friends.' Ernie continued to talk. 'We convince the people in town how we only want to protect our crops and how we are going to leave pathways to the water so the cattle can still reach the creek. Once we have the town folks on our side, we put up the wire and start having decent crops.'

'I don't know if the people in town will see our side of it,' Barlow said. 'You know how they feel about free range. It's going to look like we're taking away a sizable chunk of that range.'

Milo remained skeptical. 'Not to mention cutting off about ninety per cent of the access to the creek. It will start a range war for sure.'

'We have the right to fence our places,' Ernie was adamant. 'We all have deeds to the ground we've been working. It's the only way we are going to survive.'

'Yes, but if we fence off every farm, it will block off the creek for a half-mile or more. The cattlemen and the city folk aren't going to like that.'

'We would leave a few pathways to the water,' Ernie argued.

'What about when the Calloways drive a herd to market or come through town with a few head of horses or cattle?' Milo wanted to know. 'They will have to funnel their herd through a narrow passage or go clear around the valley.'

'What do we care?' Ernie said angrily. 'They've pushed us around since we arrived. Hardly a week goes by that some cowpuncher don't beat up on one of us farmers. I don't know a single farmer who hasn't been knocked around once or twice.'

'All the more reason we don't want to start a fullscale war,' Barlow argued, taking Milo's side.

'You're not listening to me, men,' Ernie tried to reach them again. 'We only have to get the town on our side. They proved they can stand against the ranchers and win. With them backing us up we'll have no trouble fencing off our farms.'

But Milo gave his head a negative shake. 'I don't see the people in Liberty throwing their support to our side. It was money from the ranchers that built most of the town. They helped pull most every business through during their beginning years. You can't expect those folks to suddenly turn against them.'

Before Ernie could argue his point, Barlow voiced his agreement. 'Milo's right, most of those folks owe their livelihoods to the cattlemen. They are bound to take the Calloways' side against us.'

'We need the fencing to survive!'

Ernie finally exploded. 'Can't you two get that through your heads? We either fence off our crops or we all end up broke and moving back to Ohio!'

The two men both left, shaking their heads. Ernie took a step after them but stopped. Further argument would have fallen on deaf ears.

Vince had been keeping watch on the short meeting from a short way off. Standing near the porch of the house, he had picked up a little of their conversation.

'What did they say, Pa?' he asked, already knowing the answer.

'Milo wouldn't listen to reason and Barlow usually follows his lead. Everyone is content to bury his head in the sand and continue struggling against the endless parade of wandering cattle that trample and ruin our crops. I'm tired of chasing cattle off of our land and letting a bunch of bully cowpunchers push us around.'

'Old man Cunningham has been showing me a few tricks,' Vince told

Ernie. 'You remember him telling stories about being a pugilist back in Saint Louis?'

'He was a tough man in his youth,' Ernie agreed, 'but he paid for those years of fighting. You know he can't hear out of his left ear and has almost no vision in his right eye. A man pays a heavy price for taking so many beatings.'

Vince laughed. 'Don't fret on it, Pa, I'm not learning the trade so as to become a boxer or prizefighter. I just aim to defend myself the next time one of those cow jockeys decides to push me around.'

'Fighting won't settle anything,' Ernie said.

Vince arched his brows. 'Isn't that what you were asking Milo Jackson and Hal Barlow to do, stand up and fight?'

'There wouldn't be any fight,' Ernie clarified, 'not if they would come on board with my idea. We only need to get the town behind us and the battle would be won. The sheriff and the others proved they are strong enough to stand up against the likes of Buford and Seth Calloway. They did it for the faro dealer who killed Ned.'

'Yeah, that was something,' Vince said. 'Me and Mac both arrived in town right after it happened. Everybody was talking about it. Wish we could have gotten there in time to have seen them all out there on the street, toe to toe, ready to draw down and shoot it out.'

'I don't suppose Mac Barlow can persauade his pa to come over to my way of thinking. With him on my side, we might overrule Milo's objections.'

'Ah, you know how Mac is,' Vince replied. 'He's a great kid, but when God dished him up a brain, he missed the plate with a fair portion of the serving. Mac never argues with his pa.' He uttered a cynical grunt. 'Fact is, Mac never argues with anyone. He's the only man I ever met who can stand in the middle of a fight and take both sides at the same time.'

Ernie didn't say so, but he often

thought the boy's limited thinking abilities were one of the reasons he had become Vince's best friend. His own boy was a thinker, a schemer, always the one with the bright ideas. Mac was more than satisfied to follow someone else's lead and Vince was that leader. They were a well-suited pair.

'I suppose you're right,' he admitted to Vince. 'Mac isn't the sort to stand up and tell his old man anything. He's not cut out to be a fighter.'

'Maybe not, but Mac has been my sparring partner for my pugilist training. Cunningham teaches us both at the same time.' Vince grinned. 'Next time push comes to shove betwixt us and a couple of them cow-tenders, we're going to show them a thing or two.'

'I don't want you to go looking for trouble, son,' Ernie warned. 'There are others besides Ned among the Calloway clan who don't take to losing. If you beat one of them with your fists, they are liable to grab a gun to square their differences. We can't beat them in a shooting war.'

'I hear you, Pa.' Vince dismissed his concern, 'You don't have to worry about me. I'll be careful.'

5

Paul was picking up a few items from the general store while the farmer was at the counter. He was speaking seriously yet quietly to Bryan, so his words would not be overheard. Paul did not want to eavesdrop so he kept his distance until the man had finished talking and gone out the door.

'Good morning, Bryan,' Paul greeted the storekeeper. 'Paid a visit to your wife a little bit ago.'

'She looks great don't she, Doc?'

'Everything seems fine. Another couple days and we can all breathe easier.'

'You did a great job.'

Paul shook his head. 'Give your wife the credit for being strong, tenacious and fighting to live. I'd say the baby inherited the same traits from her mother.'

Bryan laughed. 'I'm truly blessed, Doctor.'

Paul tipped his head toward the door. 'Seems you and the farmer were exchanging some serious words. I hope that doesn't mean trouble for the valley.'

Bryan sighed. 'He heard about how we stood up against the Calloways to stop them from hanging you. It gave him the impression we would do the same for him and the other farmers.'

'I thought the farmers and ranchers were getting along all right.'

'They tolerate one another but I wouldn't call it getting along. The farmers took up land along Coyote Creek so they could have easy access to the water and even use a little for irrigation. When the cattle are on this side of the mesa, the stream is the only place for cattle to water. Thirsty cattle don't pay much attention to where they are walking and often trample crops. When the corn starts to grow some of the cattle also think it's there for them to eat.'

'So much for tolerance,' Paul deduced.

'That's about the gist of it. Ernie

wants to fence off the crops to keep the cattle out. He claims they would leave openings between the fields so the cattle can get down to the water.'

'Sounds reasonable.'

Bryan grunted. 'Yeah, let's tell the Calloway clan to be reasonable and make their cattle follow a fence line until the farmers decide to put in a path to water. We can also tell them to use the mesa to start their trail herds moving, instead of bringing them down to the river first. I'm sure they won't mind.'

'Now that you put it in perspective, I do see why there is some concern.'

'Regardless of what we think, Ernie and some of the other farmers are thinking about ordering in the wire. It could start a full-scale war.'

Paul gave his head a negative shake. 'I've seen enough war to last me three lifetimes, Bryan. I sure hope it doesn't come to that.'

'Guess there isn't much you or I can do about it one way or the other.'

'You, maybe, but I don't have roots here. If it comes to a killing war, I'll pack my gear and head for Cheyenne or Denver.'

'Be a real need for a doctor should a fight start.'

Paul uttered a sigh. 'I'm not that doctor, Bryan,' he said. 'How much do I owe you for the purchase?'

Bryan scooped up the items and stuck them in a clean flour-sack. 'Not one red cent, Doc,' he told Paul. 'Long as you're looking after my Sarah, your money is no good in this store. You take whatever you need.'

'Be less expensive to pay a fee for my services.'

'I doubt you would ask for half of what any other doctor would,' Bryan replied. 'You just don't be shy about shopping here.'

'You're a good man, Bryan,' Paul told him. 'But if you and Dodge hadn't stood up to the Calloway bunch I'd have been strung up by now. Maybe you ought to figure that into the payment process.'

Bryan smiled. 'That was justice, not payment, Doc.'

Paul picked up the sack of items, raised a hand in farewell and headed out the door. It struck him that there were some good folks here in Liberty. He sure hated the idea of a bunch of them being wounded or killed in a range war.

Thinking about his conversation with Bryan, Paul considered his life's work. In his travels he had passed through several towns whose number included a doctor. He'd even passed the time with one or two during his travels. He knew why few doctors ever set up shop in out of the way places like Liberty. The reason was starvation. Money was scarce in small towns and farming communities. Customers often paid with a bushel of corn, a freshly plucked chicken or simply provided a meal and figured they were even. A man was expected to ride out in the worst of weather to deliver a baby or tend to an injury, yet he earned little more than his own satisfaction. A doctor had to run a pharmacy, sell bitters and pain-killers, often acting as the town mortician or taking odd jobs too. It was a necessity if a man wanted to live. If a doctor decided he wanted a family and home it meant moving to a larger town or city where he could actually earn a living.

So it was the issue of paying the rent and eating more than one meal a day which prompted Paul to go back to the faro table. The first night or two he had friendly players or the curious, asking questions about the procedure for delivering a baby via caesarean. On the third night a dark shadow fell over his table. He looked up to see a young man, lean and weathered from the sun . . . and who bore a striking resemblance to Ned Calloway.

'Time to step outside, Mr Killer Man,' the cowboy sneered. 'You and me have got something to settle.'

A number of patrons took notice of the challenge. Paul decided it would do no good to try and talk to the man. The boy's face was contorted in hate and if his jaw were anchored any tighter he would start breaking teeth.

With a sigh of resignation Paul closed his cash drawer and turned the lock. Mort was the only one with a key so it was secure. Then Paul followed the young cowboy out the front door and to the street.

'I'm a callin' you out!' the boy said, taking hold of his pistol butt. 'You can draw when you find the nerve.'

Slow and deliberate, Paul pulled back the sides of his jacket. 'As you can see, mister, I'm not wearing a gun.'

'He's telling the truth, Lester,' a nearby cowboy spoke up. 'The dude don't wear a gun.'

Lester's face grew red with rage. 'You ain't getting out of this that easy, Killer Man! You done kilt my brother and you're gonna pay!'

'You don't need a gun to get the job done, Lester!' one of his friends called. 'Knock his head off!'

Lester quickly unbuckled his gunbelt and handed his six-gun to the cowboy who had spoken.

Paul removed his jacket and draped it over the nearest hitching-rail. Before he could step up to meet Lester an elderly gent came forward.

'Best be protecting those hands, Doctor,' he said, holding out a pair of buckskin gloves 'These will save you breaking a knuckle . . . ' adding with a grin, 'if you manage to hit your opponent.'

Paul slipped on the snug-fitting gloves and took a deep breath. He had done some fighting back in his college days, but that was years ago. Lester was young and eager, possibly too eager, so Paul hoped that that would work in his favor. Even as he sized up his adversary he was thinking of how to avoid hurting the young man.

Lester Calloway waited until Paul stepped into the human ring which had been formed by the spectators. He rushed at Paul swinging like an enraged demon, throwing punches as fast as he could.

Ducking and blocking, Paul prevented most of Lester's punches from finding a mark. He caught one blow high on his head, several landed against his forearms and shoulders and one clipped him in the cheek.

The explosion lasted for several seconds, but Lester quickly ran out of steam. When he drew up short trying to recoup his strength, Paul slipped inside his guard and drove a fist into his solar plexus.

Lester had been sucking for wind and the punch drove what little air he had left from his lungs. He half-folded at the middle, paralyzed by the blow. Paul could have pounded him severely about the face, possibly even knocked him unconscious. Instead, Paul backed off and gave him a chance to gulp down several swallows of air.

When the youngster came at him a second time, Paul used the same tactic. He let the boy swing away, expending his energy and not doing much damage. Then when his strength started to fade, he moved in close and landed another punishing blow to his mid-section. Lester grunted from the pain and air rushed from his lungs. He folded over as his legs nearly buckled beneath him. He staggered backwards and cowered defensively, his fists raised to protect his face, elbows tucked to guard his ribs and stomach. He expected an attack that would certainly win the fight.

Paul ignored the yells from the crowd to knock the boy down. The last thing he wanted was a second Calloway grudge against him. He held back and lowered his guard.

'I'm about done in, kid,' he lied. 'You sure enough handed me a thrashing.'

Lester swallowed a gulp of air and lifted his head. His eyes betrayed his fears — he realized Paul could have handed him a thorough whipping. However, the unexpected surrender gave him an opening to save face.

'You done kilt my brother,' Lester said, his voice still weak from lack of air. 'You deserved a beating.'

Paul held his hands up, palms outward, admitting defeat. 'I'm real sorry about Ned,' he told the boy seriously. 'I wish I could have only wounded him but he was too fast on the draw. I threw the shot in desperation, trying only to keep from being killed.'

Lester lifted his chin, his strength and pride returning. 'You were lucky, faro dealer. Ned was mighty good with a gun. If you'd have been wearing a gun in a holster, he'd have kilt you for sure.'

'No argument from me on that point, Mr Calloway. Had it been a square draw Ned would be alive today instead of me.'

Lester seemed to enjoy being spoken to with respect and having a title in front of his name. He regained his wind but showed no desire to engage in continuing the fight. Instead, he ducked his head and uttered a sigh. 'I should have been at the casino to stop him,' he said with some remorse. 'Ned always was a hot-tempered sort.'

'It's a shame you weren't in town, Mr Calloway.'

Lester bobbed his head. 'Reckon this scrap is over.' He took a step but paused to look at Paul one last time. 'You gave as good as you got, Warrick,' he admitted, displaying a degree of maturity. 'I suspect you won't have no more trouble from us Calloways.'

'I appreciate that,' Paul remained sincere, 'and I am real sorry about Ned.'

Lester walked off into the darkness, followed by a couple other cowboys. The crowd broke up with more than a few mutterings about what a lame fight they had just witnessed.

Paul removed the buckskin gloves as the old-timer moved over to confront him.

'If I'd known you weren't going to do no more than dance with young Lester, I'd have saved giving you my sparring gloves.'

Paul grinned, wincing at a sudden tightness above his left eye.

'Come on,' the old boy said. 'I've got a block of ice stored in my shed. I'll chip you off a piece to help stop the swelling of that eye.'

'Much obliged, Mr . . . ?'

'Cunningham,' the man answered, 'but most call me Pugs.'

'Pugs, I'm Paul Warrick.'

'Guess you don't have to tell me your name, sonny. You've made yourself the topic of conversation at near every waterhole and beer-selling place in town. I've been putting off getting a shave and haircut 'cause the barber don't want to talk about nothing else but you.'

'I'm surprised you want to offer me some ice.'

The gent showed him a crooked grin. 'One of the few teeth I've got left has been giving me hell lately. I figured if I befriended you it might be worth a look.'

'Faro dealer, surgeon, boxer and now

dentist,' Paul said with a shake of his head. 'Next thing I'll be shoeing horses!'

* * *

Buford cast a hard look at Lester when he came through the door.

'Where you been, boy?' he wanted to know. 'Your ma went to bed two hours ago.'

'You didn't have to wait up for me, Pa. I'm not a kid any more.'

Buford snorted. 'You're my only child living at home. Guess I can worry about you if I've a mind to.'

Lester removed his hat and hung it on the deer-antler coat-rack near the door. When he turned around he could see his father was not going to turn in for the night until he told him the truth.

'I ran into that faro dealing medico in town,' Lester began. 'I had a mind to gut shoot him and watch him die in a pool of his own blood.' He had Buford's complete attention now. 'It didn't come to gunplay,' he explained quickly, 'as the doc warn't carrying no shooting iron.'

'So what happened?'

Lester showed him the backs of his hands. The knuckles were swollen and scraped from the number of punches he had bounced off of the doctor's forearms and shoulders. 'I fought him fair and square out on the main street in front of Gastone's place.'

Buford moved over and did a quick examination of his boy's hands. Then he studied his unmarked face.

'You must be a whole lot better with your fists than I ever give you credit for, son. It don't look as if that murdering dude landed a single punch!'

Lester sighed from the weight of the truth. 'He took the pounding I give him and only hit me back twice.'

'That thar sounds like a thorough beatin', it sure do!'

Lester gave his head a negative shake. 'He could have taken me, Pa,' he admitted. 'He knocked the wheels off 'n my wagon both times he hit me, but he didn't follow up and finish the job. He let me win the fight.' With a grunt: 'shucks, he called an end to the contest whilst I was bent at the middle and gasping for breath. He could have knocked me into next week, but he allowed everyone watching to think I had beaten him.'

'Shows he's genuinely skeered of us, boy.'

Lester laughed his contempt. 'I've seen skeered a few times, Pa. That fellow warn't skeered, not by a long shot.'

'Then why . . . ?'

'I guess he didn't want us for enemies,' Lester deduced. 'He did his best not to hurt me none and then told the crowd I had won the fight.'

'You think he's up to something? Maybe he is trying to make us look weak to the farmers or something.'

'I'd say he did the only thing he could, Pa. If I had knocked him down I might have stomped him to death. If he had beaten me, Tom or some of the boys would have evened the score. No, I'm for thinkin' that dude showed me that he could have whupped me good, but he accepted the loss to end the fight betwixt him and us.'

'All right, I'll accept your thinkin' on this here fracas.'

'I'd like for you to accept something else, Pa.'

'And what would that be?'

'That we're done fighting with him. I told him as much.'

Buford's face darkened with a scowl. 'You had no right to tell him that.'

'He apologized more than once for being forced to kill Ned,' Lester told him. 'He said Ned was so quick to get his gun out that he just fired off a shot to stop him. The man might be a fast talker, but I believe he was telling the truth. Word around town is that he don't never carry a gun. Killing Ned was a lucky shot by the doc, that's all it was.'

Buford slowly simmered to a medium

boil. He knew Lester was telling the story straight. And Seth believed the doc had saved Roper's daughter and grandchild. He had even overheard his wife talking about it to his daughter-in-law. The pain of losing Ned still burned a raging fire in his chest, but he had to accept his boy was dead and nothing would change that.

'I'll abide by your word, son,' he said after a brief argument with himself. 'Far as it goes with the faro dealer, the matter of Ned's death is settled.'

★ ★ ★

Jenny waited for her mother to wring out the shirt so the basket would be full. Friday was laundry day at the Calloway house. It took several hours to wash all of the clothes for the five of them. She was thankful her mother did the actual washing. It wasn't out of the goodness of her heart, more that Iris didn't trust Jenny to get the last speck of dirt from a shirt or pair of trousers.

Jenny had done the washing part before and hated the way the home-made lye soap left her hands red and tender for several days. After such a chore she would have been ashamed to have a man try and hold her hand. She much preferred the hanging out of clothes to the endless grind of using the scrub-board and working her hands raw.

'Nelda was telling me Sarah named her little girl Paulette.' Iris broke a long silence. 'Named after the man who killed Ned, ain't that so?'

'Yes, Ma.'

Iris didn't look up from her work, pausing to hold up Andrew's shirt, examining it for any lurking particle of dirt or grime. Finding none she proceeded to wring the water out and passed it to Jenny.

'Ken was saying you done passed the time of day with that killer whilst you were in town.'

Jenny hid the involuntary flinch, while placing the shirt in the clothes' basket. Withholding any emotion she replied, 'It was before I learned he was the man who had killed Ned, Ma.' When her mother said nothing, she took up for the man's defense.

'It does sound as if it Ned was at fault for getting himself shot. Over a dozen men in town saw the whole thing. Way the story goes, Ned had been doing a lot of hard drinking and gambled away all of his money. He got sore about losing and started the fight. He didn't give the doctor a way out. He forced the gunfight and died from a single shot.'

'Are you sticking up for the killer of my nephew?'

'I'm only stating what I've heard about the shooting,' Jenny said. Then with a trace of ire: 'Besides which, cousin or not, Ned was a blowhard bully, Ma. He constantly tormented me and was always trying to peek up my skirt or down my blouse. It was no better for Ken. Ned pushed him around and bullied him for as long as I can remember. Ned was ornery and mean, especially when he was drinking.'

'I recollect he could be a troublesome kid growing up too,' Iris admitted, carefully inspecting a wet apron. 'Reckon Buford never took a strap to him often enough to bring him into line. It ain't always the fault of the father, but Buford sure didn't help the situation none.'

'I never wanted to see Ned hurt or killed,' Jenny said quickly, 'but he was the one who started the fight. I'm sorry he's dead, but he was aiming to kill Mr Warrick, whether he fought back or not.'

'Ned was drunk,' Iris countered. 'Too bad your doctor friend couldn't have found another way to settle their differences.'

'Ned didn't offer him a choice, Ma. Those who saw it claim Ned drew his gun intending to kill Mr Warrick. The doctor managed to shoot first. Everyone saw it.'

Iris wrung out the apron and dropped it into the nearly full laundry basket. Jenny picked it up to take out to the line but her mother stopped her.

'Tell me, Jen, why was a medical doctor dealing faro in the casino?'

'I don't know.'

'With the shortage of doctors out in this part of the country, why would a trained medico take to working for Gaston?'

'It's a mystery to me. Like I told you, when I met him I didn't know he was the one who had killed Ned.'

'What did you talk about?'

'Nothing much.'

Iris lifted her eyes from her work. 'This here doctor, he an older gent?'

'About Tom's age — late twenties, I would guess.'

'Um,' Iris murmured under her breath.

Jenny recognized the cynical tone. 'What?' she asked.

'This doctor, I'm thinking he ain't exactly the cull of the herd.'

Jenny sighed. 'You sound like Ken. He tried using the same ploy on me.'

'Ploy?' Iris repeated the unfamiliar

word. 'What in tarnation is a ploy?'

Jenny was about to explain when the front door suddenly flew open!

Two of the ranch wranglers, Jingo and Sage, appeared on the porch. Jingo was carrying Jenny's young nephew, Billy, in his arms. Billy was the eldest of Tom and Dora's three children, a month short of being seven years old.

Jenny set the basket on the floor and hurried over to see what had happened. Ken, who had been working at the corral, came through the door behind the two hired hands. Between Ken's look of dread and the tear-streaks down Billy's cheeks, Jenny feared the worst.

Jingo placed the boy down on a chair at the dining table and Iris gently moved his shirtsleeve aside so she could look at his arm. Billy was doing his best not to cry, but tears filled his eyes and his teeth were clenched against the pain. It took only a glance to see he had broken his arm.

'It didn't seem dangerous,' Sage lamented. 'One minute he's up on the fence, watching us break a horse and the next — '

'Damn loco-wild horse!' Jingo swore, slamming his fist into the open palm of his other hand. 'Worthless mustang rammed up against the fence with me trying to knock me out of the saddle. The jolt caused Billy to lose his balance. He fell backward off of the top rail and landed on his left arm.'

'The bone is poking through the skin,' Jenny's mother said quietly, her voice trembling with regret. Her eyelids squeezed tightly together for a single moment preventing tears from forming. 'Just like Joe Bass,' she murmured in dismay. 'Busted Billy's arm almost the exact same way.'

Jenny sucked in her breath. Joe Bass had worked for them one summer and broke his arm when he took a nasty fall from a green-broke horse. The bone had protruded through the skin after his accident and they had taken him over to Gillette where there was a doctor. The man took one look at the injury and announced that amputation was the only way to save his life. Seth paid the doctor for the chore and gave the hired hand a horse and three months' wages. It was the last they ever saw of Joe Bass.

'Where are Tom and Buford?' Jenny asked.

'They're up on the mesa with Lester and some others,' the bronco buster answered. 'It will probably take a couple hours to find them.'

'You go fetch them, Sage,' Iris told the older wrangler. 'If you see Seth or either of my other boys send them this way too.'

'Yes, ma'am,' he replied. Then he raced out the door to get his horse.

'Can you fix it, Aunt Iris?' little Billy asked, his small face contorted by pain and fear. 'It sure hurts.'

'You just sit back and rest your arm on the table,' she suggested softly. 'I'll wrap a bandage over it real gentle to help stop the bleeding.'

He was unable to stifle a whimper.

'It's bad, ain't it?'

'It's a man-sized injury, Billy. You just have to be brave. Soon as your pa arrives we'll decide the best way to tend to your arm.'

Jenny grabbed up her hat. 'Jingo,' she said to the horse wrangler, 'I need a horse and I need it right now!'

'You got it,' Jingo replied. 'Lady is in the corral. I was going to give her new shoes this afternoon. I'll have her saddled in two shakes of a calf's tail.'

As he raced out the door, Iris regarded her with a curious look. 'Where you off to, Jen?'

'To fetch the doctor from town, Mama,' she answered. 'He saved Sarah and her baby from dying.'

'The doctor at Gillette didn't do much good for Joe Bass.'

'Doctor Warrick is different!' Jenny declared. 'I met him; I know he cares. That over-the-hill medico in Gillette barely gave Joe's injury a glance. This is Billy we're talking about. I want a professional opinion from someone other than that butcher!'

Iris frowned her concern. 'Seth and Buford might not hold with having that man in our house.'

Ken spoke up before Jen could argue. 'I'll take responsibility, Ma,' he declared. 'If there's any objections, I'll take the heat. Billy's arm needs fixing and Liberty is a whole lot closer than Gillette. Let Sis ride for the doctor.'

Iris gave a nod of her head. 'Be careful and hurry back, Jen. If the men show up before you return, I'll stall them as long as I can.'

Jenny didn't hesitate. She flew out the door, hoping Jingo had somehow magically gotten Lady saddled and ready. The big mare was a strong horse and had plenty of wind. Jenny hoped the steed was ready, because the ride ahead was going to be the fastest and hardest of her life.

6

Paul left Sarah and the baby after checking them both for any problems. He was relieved that mother and daughter were doing just fine. As he started across the street a female voice shouted out his name. He stopped, looked up the street and recognized Jenny Calloway sitting atop a lathered horse. She bore down on him at a gallop as if she intended to run him down. For the briefest moment he thought she might be bent on avenging the killing of Ned.

However, she pulled up a few feet before trampling him under the hoofs of her mount. He stepped to one side as she swung a leg over the saddle and slid to the ground. Curious as he was, he did not miss the glimpse of smooth white leg exposed by her actions. She was not dressed for riding, clad instead in an ordinary house-dress.

'I'm glad I found you!' she said breathlessly. Then she stopped speaking and stared at him.

'What happened to your face?'

'My face?'

'It looks as if you've been in a fight.'

Paul frowned. 'I wondered about that when I shaved this morning. I couldn't figure out why my vision was blurred. Did you say I've been in a fight?'

Jenny didn't intend to play games. 'Tom's boy fell off of a fence and broke his arm,' she informed him sharply. 'The bone is sticking out through the skin!'

While Paul had not practiced his medical training for several years, he had continued to glean information and peruse new procedures which were written up in the latest medical journals. Some of the articles had been devastating to his conscience, because he learned how his ignorance had cost many men their limbs and possibly even their lives.

He hesitated for a moment and scrutinized the girl. She could be the bait for a trap. Once away from town, he might find a rope and tree-branch had been designated for his neck. However, Lester had said there would be no more trouble with his family.

'Are you sure you want my help?' he asked. 'You do know I'm the man who killed your cousin?'

'Yes, no thanks to you!' she declared. 'You neglected to mention that bit of information when we first met.'

'I should have told you,' he admitted. Then he asked: 'Knowing the truth now, why would you trust me with one of your kin?'

'Killer or not, I saw you with Sarah and the baby,' Jenny answered quickly. 'I know you care about your patients. And . . . ' she swallowed against a wave of emotion, 'Billy's a sweet little boy. If you could only . . . '

Paul didn't force her to continue. 'My bag is at the hotel,' he said. 'It would save time if you could go to the livery and tell the hostler to saddle my horse.'

'I need to trade Lady for another mount too,' Jenny responded. She quickly swung up onto her horse Indian-style and looked down at him. 'I'll have them both ready to ride in five minutes,' she promised.

Paul caught a second glimpse of bare leg from her unorthodox manner of mounting. However, he stuck the mental image in the back of his mind. He would dwell on the young woman's appealing qualities when there was more time. Presently, he needed to tend to a young patient, the nephew of the man he had killed.

By the time Paul had retrieved his bag and made his way to the livery his saddled horse was being led out by the hostler. The old boy grinned as he approached.

'I'd have gotten Jenny another steed too, but she shoved me out of the way. Said I was too danged slow.'

Jenny appeared at that moment,

leading a sturdy-looking sorrel. She stopped the horse long enough to tighten the saddle cinch one last time before she climbed aboard. Making an effort to keep her skirt covering as much leg as possible, she paused to glare down at the hostler.

'If this blasted hay-burner held her breath so the saddle turns with me, I'll swap her to the first hungry Indians I can find.'

'Sally won't let you down, Miss Calloway,' the easy-going gent replied. 'You kin trust me on thet.'

Paul attached his bag behind the saddle and mounted his horse. As he didn't know the way to the Calloway spread, he let the girl lead the way. She did so at a gallop, thundering out of town with her horse showing more speed than he would have expected.

He was on the better horse but Jenny was the more experienced rider. She got three or four miles out of the rental mare before she slowed the pace to a walk. Both mounts were heaving and puffing by that time.

'How much farther is it?' Paul asked, moving up alongside.

'Another coupla miles. I'll give this bag of bones a couple minutes to catch her breath and then we'll set out at a lope. We ought to make it in fifteen minutes or so.'

'You do realize I'm not a practicing doctor?' he said. 'I mean, I was a surgeon during the war, but I haven't done anything since.'

She cast a sidelong glance at him. He could read the questions in her make-up but she stated simply: 'You saved Sarah and her baby.'

'Only if Sarah doesn't develop infection.' He cautioned her optimism.

Jenny lowered her head. 'We had a hired man who broke his arm back a couple seasons,' she informed him gravely. 'We took him to a medico in Gillette. The doctor took one look at the bone sticking out and cut off his arm. I don't know what happened to the poor man after that.'

'Amputation for a compound fracture has been the standard for years,' Paul admitted. 'During the war . . . ' He was unable to finish. The memories were too vivid, the images which assailed his mind too horrific. He had to block the mental visions or he knew he could do nothing for the injured party.

Jenny did not ask why he had not finished, but did take notice of his being unarmed.

'You don't carry a gun?' she asked.

'I have one in my saddle-bags, should the need arise. I'm not a very good shot.'

'You did all right the night you killed Ned!'

'House rules at the casino,' he was matter-of-fact. 'Gaston harbors some concern that anyone could walk in and rob his dealers. Had I been more proficient with the weapon, I might have only wounded Ned.'

'Why hide the truth the day we met?' she asked. 'Why didn't you tell me you were the one who killed Ned?'

'I'm not proud to have taken a man's life. The act of shooting Ned was nothing more than my natural instinct for self-preservation. Had I been allowed to think about it first, I probably would have let him kill me.'

'If he had killed you, what would have happened to Sarah and Paulette?'

He was surprised at her reasoning. 'Are you defending my action against your cousin?'

'Merely stating a fact,' she retorted. 'If Ned had killed you at the casino, those two would have died too.'

'Even so, I wish I had been a better shot and only wounded him.'

'Come on,' Jenny said, nudging her horse to a faster pace, 'you can redeem yourself with one of Ned's brothers by helping his little boy.'

Paul touched his horse's ribs with his heels and his steed broke into an easy lope. The notion of what lay ahead caused an onrush of dread. He was assailed by mental pictures from the past, horrible, ghastly recollections that ripped and shredded his sanity. Firming his resolve, he forcibly suppressed the onslaught of terrible memories and images of carnage and suffering. To avoid a crippling depression, he concentrated on the girl leading the way. She rode with the ease of a Sioux warrior, one with the horse, urging more speed out of her rented mount. Seeking a deterrent to his dark memories, he took notice of how Jenny's dress rode up above her knees. Also, the act of leaning forward in the saddle caused the snug material to prominently exhibit her feminine attributes. Jenny was nubile, attractive and an altogether charming young lady. She would make some lucky man a very good wife.

⋆　⋆　⋆

Two men came out to the porch to welcome the new arrivals at the Calloway house: a man Paul didn't know and Jenny's brother, Ken. Paul pulled his horse to a stop and dismounted alongside Jenny. He glanced at the pair, expecting either a cool greeting or a get-the-hell-out-of-here warning. However, concern for the injured boy showed more clearly on their faces than contempt for the man who had killed one of their number.

An elderly woman appeared at the doorway and gently nudged the two men to either side. She appraised Paul with a critical eye and addressed him with a blunt proclamation.

'You got a real shiner there, sonny. I'd say someone didn't like your looks.'

'And me being such a nice guy too,' Paul replied with a careful smile.

'Jenny tells me you're a doctor.' The woman turned to business.

'I've had some experience as a surgeon,' he replied carefully, reaching up behind the saddle to free his small satchel.

The woman waited until he squared around to face her again. She appeared both sagacious and formidable for a woman of such short stature. He paused a moment to meet her gaze on a level plane. The etched features of her expression did not change, but there appeared a grim acceptance within her eyes.

'Follow me,' she ordered and led the way into the darkened house.

'I'll take your horse,' the stranger on the porch offered. 'Yours too, Miss Jenny.'

'Thanks, Jingo,' she said and looked around quickly. 'No sign of Tom or Dad?'

'They are probably on their way down from the mesa,' Ken answered. 'I'd bet Sage has found them by this time.'

Paul's eyes adjusted to the darker interior of the house as he passed through a comfortable-looking sitting room and went forward to the kitchen. A little boy was seated at the dining table with his arm propped up on a pillow. A piece of cloth was draped over his arm and blood had soaked through, enough to leave a small crimson blotch on the material.

'So, big fella,' he spoke to the boy, 'they tell me you had a little mishap this morning.'

'Uh-huh,' the boy replied through quivering lips. His eyes were red and a bit swollen from crying, but he was trying hard to act like a man. Then seeing Paul's eye he said. 'Looks like you had one of them there mishaps too.'

'Yes, silly me, I wasn't looking where I was going and ran headlong into a man's fist. It's lucky the other fellow didn't hurt his hand.'

The boy gave him a half-smile.

Paul moved up to the table and gently lifted up the cloth. 'Let's have a peek,' he said, careful to hide any emotion.

The white of the bone was thrust through a portion of angry red flesh, but it looked to be a relatively clean break. He began to examine the injury, but the sight caused an immediate onrush of memories to wash over his consciousness. He could hear the wail of terrible screams, his senses were assailed by the smell of blood and he was immediately surrounded by a dark shroud of ghastly, lingering death. Paul clenched his teeth and swallowed hard, battling against the flood of dreadful sensations.

Show some bravado, you spineless poltroon! he castigated himself sternly and sucked in a silent, deep breath to combat the overwhelming images.

With a steadfast resolution he fixed his sight on the boy's small face. The child had his teeth set against any sudden pain, while his eyes were hopeful, expectant — a child's innocent confidence that a doctor would make everything better. He battled for control, fearful that the images would overwhelm his consciousness.

'What do you think?' The elderly woman's calm voice shattered the viselike grip of the brutal memories. His head cleared instantly and he was back in control.

Paul steadied his focus and examined the break more closely. He mentally reviewed the in-depth article describing the delicate procedure he had read about in the medical journal. This appeared to be a prime example, the very sort of injury described.

'It's a pretty nasty break,' he said at last to the woman.

'We had a hired man with much the same kind of injury,' the woman spoke softly to Paul. 'The doctor in Gillette said there was nothing he could do to save the arm.'

'Until recently it has been the standard procedure to remove the limb to prevent infection that could cost the person's life.'

She regarded him with a penetrating gaze. 'You said until recently?'

Paul was aware of the anxious faces surrounding him and the boy. He took a deep breath before he spoke, attempting to exude a calm and professional demeanor.

'According to the recent medical journals, there has been some success with cleansing the break and resetting the broken bone. The prevention of infection is of paramount importance, but the study cases confirm that the bone will mend the same as a simple fracture.'

'You've never done or seen this operation before?' the woman asked.

'It's a new revelation that has only begun to gain acceptance in medicine,' he told her. 'And no, I've never seen it performed, I've only read about it.'

The woman flashed a glance at Jenny then put a tender gaze upon the little boy. When she spoke, it sounded as if she were uttering a prayer.

'With the Lord's help, we'll see this through, won't we, Billy?' The boy managed a nod and the woman turned to Paul and asked: 'What do you need from us?'

'I'll need a place where the boy can lie down,' he began. 'Also, I need some hot water and an exceptionally clean cloth for a dressing.' He shifted his attention to Ken Calloway. 'I'll need two splints, wide as the boy's arm, flat on one side and about . . . ' he held up his hands to show the measurement, 'this long.'

'You got it, Doc!' Ken responded. 'I'll have them ready for you in ten or fifteen minutes.'

Paul surveyed the others and returned to the woman of the house. 'Madam,' he said, 'I'll need you to administer chloroform to the boy. He'll have to be unconscious for me to clean and set his arm. Everyone else will have to leave the room. We don't want to risk infection.'

Jenny frowned at his selecting her mother. She had been the one to go get him and now he was ordering her to leave. The logic of his choosing Iris because of her calm and experience in doctoring minor injuries was obvious but it still hurt. She backed up a step, ready to turn and leave the room.

'Jenny.' Iris stopped her. 'Put a kettle of water on the stove and fetch me the cloth I brought home to make dinner napkins. It's the cleanest piece of material we have in the house.'

Thankful to have a chance to help, Jenny hurried to do her bidding.

'Once the boy's arm is set, he will need to stay in bed for a few days. We can't allow any unnecessary movement that might interrupt the healing process.'

'I understand, Doctor.'

'All right, young man,' Paul said, offering a professional smile to Billy, 'let's take care of that arm so you can get back to playing again.'

⋆　⋆　⋆

Jenny was outside on the porch with Ken when Buford and several others arrived. Tom was first to reach the door, but Jenny moved quickly to block his way.

'No, Tom!' she told him firmly. 'No one is to go in until the doctor has finished.'

'That's my son!' he snapped.

She held her ground. 'You want him to have the best chance of mending, don't you?'

Tom placed his hands on Jenny's shoulders ready to push her bodily aside.

'The doc says fear of infection is the reason they took Joe Bass's arm, Tom.' Ken spoke up, stepping over to stand at his sister's side. 'One speck of dust is all it takes. No one is allowed in but Ma and she is the one helping with the chloroform.'

Tom reluctantly let go of Jenny and backed up. He looked around quickly. 'Where is Dora?'

'Jingo went to fetch your wife. They ought to be back here at any minute.'

'Does Seth know about this?' Buford demanded an answer. 'Does he know the man who kilt my boy is right here in his own house?'

Ken shook his head. 'Andrew and Pa are checking the herd over on the south range. It would take all day to find them.'

Buford anchored his teeth and grew red in the face, resisting the effort not to yell an obscenity and charge into the house.

'The man is trying to save your grandson's arm, Uncle Buford.' Jenny attempted to calm the man's rage. 'Would you prefer we take him to Gillette? You remember what the medico there did for Joe Bass — he cut off his arm!'

'Jenny's right,' Tom told his father quietly. 'No matter what else has happened, we can't interfere. If there's any chance at all of saving my boy's arm . . . '

Tom's voice became blocked with emotion. He didn't have to finish the sentence and Buford didn't push the issue. Instead, he turned and looked off toward the next hill. A mile beyond the crest of that hill was his ranch.

'Ma and Doris ought to be here by now,' he said presently, accepting the situation. 'I swear that Jingo sometimes moves with all the speed of a wind-broke mule.'

'I see dust!' Jenny exclaimed, pointing at the distant trail. 'They're coming.'

'Must be in the wagon,' Tom said. 'Guess Mom is bringing the kids.'

'Going to be a dozen of us sitting here on the porch waiting on that faro-dealing doctor,' Ken observed aloud. 'Sure hope the man knows what he's doing.'

* * *

By the time Billy regained his awareness, his arm was bandaged, tightly encased in splints and suspended in a sling from the overhead bunk. This was where Ken and Andrew had slept, the upper bunk for Ken, the lower for Andrew. With Andrew now married, Ken had the room to himself.

Paul explained the situation to Billy. He was still groggy, but gave a nod that he understood. After a few moments he went back to sleep.

'This accident took a lot out of him,' Iris told Paul.

'Be nice if he would sleep about twenty hours a day,' Paul replied. 'A little boy has a lot of energy. It's going to be tough on him to lie there with his arm in a stationary sling.'

'We'll keep him company and play games. He's right-handed, so he can still play checkers or a game of cards.'

Paul began to put away his medical supplies.

'Three days?' Iris asked, making certain she remembered the instructions.

'I believe if you are very careful the boy can be transported home in about three days. We don't want any avoidable jarring to the arm, so you will have to see to it that he makes the trip with the least amount of bumps or jolts. I'll be out to check on him tomorrow and we'll know more then.'

'You seem very caring for a man who killed my nephew in a gunfight.'

There was no animosity in her voice,

only a curious tone. Paul gave his shoulders a shrug.

'I didn't have time to think about it,' he replied carefully. 'Ned was angry about losing his money and wanted a fight. I offered to stake him to another game but he wasn't of a mind to listen. When he drew his gun, I instinctively grabbed the one in the cash drawer and shot him.'

'Ned was always on the wild side,' Iris admitted. 'Truth be told, I'm surprised he lived as long as he did.'

Paul had his things stowed back in the medical bag. He handed Iris a bottle. 'If the pain gets too bad for the boy, give him a sip of this. No more than a sip every few hours today and one at bedtime. If he's careful and only moves the arm with the utmost care it ought to heal. As for the pain, I doubt he should need the medicine after today, except maybe at bedtime to help him sleep.'

'I understand.'

Sucking in a deep breath for the

courage to face the boy's relatives, Paul walked through the house to the front door. He stepped out to a sea of anxious faces. The eldest of the group displayed more than anxiety: his was a hostile glare.

'How is he?' Jenny asked, before anyone else had a chance to speak.

'Did you save the arm?' Ken joined in with his own question.

Before everyone started talking at once, Paul lifted his free hand for silence.

'I want to be completely honest with you folks,' he began. 'The procedure I performed is something I have only read about in a medical journal. If the boy develops an infection the arm will have to be sacrificed to save his life.' He let the words sink in before continuing. 'For the next few days the boy must be kept as immobile as possible, no jarring, twisting or use of his injured left arm whatsoever. It would only take a slight movement to dislodge the bone and the mending process would have to start all over again.'

'I'm Billy's father,' Tom spoke up. 'Do you think he's gonna be all right?'

'The procedure has been proven sound,' Paul replied, 'but we'll have to give it a few days and see. I'll check in daily until we are confident there is no infection. If we pass that first obstacle, then the bone only has to mend, same as an ordinary fracture.'

'You done killed my eldest son!' Buford said testily, his jaw thrust out, eyes burning with a desire to dismantle Paul like a cheap toy. 'I hate trusting you with my grandson's welfare.'

'Had I had been a better shot, Mr Calloway, I might have only wounded your son. I have not had enough experience with a gun to do more than point and shoot. I am more regretful for his death than I can ever put into words.'

Buford continued to glare, but showed no tendency to get physical. 'Lester said he give you a coupla good shots,' he referred to the fight. 'I see he pert'near closed your one eye.'

'Yes, it's lucky I could see well enough to tend to the boy.'

The man let out a breath, as if he had been holding it, and gave a tilt of his head toward the house. 'If you save my grandson's arm,' he said thickly, 'I'll maybe rethink having you strung up.'

'I hope to save his arm for the sake of his own future, not to save my own neck,' Paul replied, but added quickly: 'however, I do appreciate the senti-ment.'

Jingo came forward leading his horse. 'I watered your bronc so he'd ready to ride. We need to return a wagon to town and exchange a couple of our own animals — Jenny's mare included. If you see the hostler tell him we'll be by tomorrow to straighten everything out.'

Paul nodded his assurance and went over to his horse. Most of the others hurried inside to visit with Billy, but Jenny remained on the porch.

'I'll cross my fingers for Billy,' she said. 'And I hope you can stay out of further trouble.'

Paul mounted the horse and smiled down at her. 'I appreciate the thought.'

'I could have ridden into town as a ruse to get you out here alone,' she pointed out. 'Buford would like to see you dead.'

'The thought crossed my mind,' he admitted.

'But you came. Why?'

'You.'

She frowned at the simple answer. 'Me?'

He grinned wider. 'Once you rode in wearing that snug-fitting house-dress, I would have blissfully followed you to my grave.'

A trace of crimson entered her otherwise sun-kissed complexion but, instead of being embarrassed or offended, a slight smile skipped playfully along her lips.

'I wondered how come that nag from the livery stable was able to stay ahead of your mount. Now I know you were only studying my . . . ' she hesitated, then finished, 'my riding style.'

'Guilty as charged,' he concurred.

'I've a couple brothers who would black your other eye for looking at me in an improper way.'

Paul chuckled. 'And, if you'll pardon my frankness, I believe the ride here would be well worth the beating.'

Jenny had no comeback for that remark. Instead of speaking again she merely raised a hand in farewell.

Paul started back for town. He would have enjoyed a prolonged visit with Jenny, but there were still high fences between himself and the Calloways. They might be inclined to forgive him somewhat for Ned's death if Billy's arm healed. At present, it was the best chance Paul had to start the mending.

7

It was the second meeting concerning barbed wire. Ernie again pleaded his case, reiterating how desperately they needed to protect their crops from the wandering cattle.

'We can't do it,' Milo argued, when he had said his piece. 'You admitted we need the town on our side and we all figured the killing of Ned would bring them to our corner. But it hasn't worked out that way. Did you know Warrick went out and tended to Tom Calloway's boy? The day after his fight with Lester and the man went out there and saved the boy's arm. We all figured the new doctor would be on our side and he would sway some of the folks from town. Well, it isn't going to happen that way.'

'I'm afraid Milo's right,' Hal Barlow agreed. 'Instead of the doc being a catalyst for our side, he's made peace and reunited the town with the Calloway ranches. We are in this alone again.'

'Alone or not, we need to take action. We can't get through another hard winter without producing decent crops. Between what they stomp on and what they eat, those mangy cattle are taking the food right out of our children's mouths.'

'No one is in disagreement with you, Ernie,' Milo told him, 'but we can't stop the cattle from watering along the creek. It's the only water for miles around.'

'I keep telling you, we'll leave openings for the cattle. They will learn to use the trails between our fields.'

'It isn't what the cattle will do or not do, Ernie,' Milo countered, 'it's what the ranchers will do. I suspect the cattle can be taught to use a narrow passage between our planted fields, but how are you going to sell that idea to the Calloway families?'

'We could do it, if we go before them united, with the sheriff and a few of the town citizens — maybe the doctor too.'

'You could be right, Ernie,' Milo allowed. 'If you can get those people on board, I'll join your plan.' He pointed a bony finger at Ernie, 'but if you can't get them to co-operate, my answer is still no.'

'Milo speaks for me too,' Hal added.

'I'll talk to them,' Ernie said, unable to hide his eagerness. 'I'm pretty sure we can get Bryan, Kip, the sheriff and maybe Mort Gaston. As for the doctor, he will be eager to prevent any kind of war. Would that suit you?'

'I'll go you one better, Ernie,' Milo said. 'You get four out of the five to come along and I'll join you.'

'Me too,' Hal chipped in.

Ernie said farewell and watched his neighbors leave. Vince looked over from where he was fixing a broken harness strap for the plow horse. There was an unasked question on his son's face, but Ernie simply raised a hand, a sign not to stop his chore as there had been no change as yet.

Meanwhile, he was turning over ideas and trying to decide the best way to approach the town's people. The sheriff could be swayed without much effort and Bryan had always lamented the lack of peaceful coexistence between the farmers and the ranchers. Mort would follow the money path, and bigger and better crops meant more spending money for everyone in the valley. As for the doctor, he was bound to support a project that would prevent a range war. It seemed fortune had at last begun to smile on the farmers.

★   ★   ★

Two weeks had passed and Billy's arm was healing nicely. Paul stopped by to check on the boy's progress every couple days and the reception was reserved but cordial. The one odd coincidence was that Jenny happened to be visiting with Tom's family or arrived before he left, each time he checked on Billy. She was present when Paul had the boy do some simple arm exercises. There was no pain and he had use of the full range of movements.

'I believe he's going to be fine,' he announced to Tom's wife. 'Keep the splints in place for another two weeks for safety's sake, but the puncture wound has completely healed. I believe he's going to be as good as new.'

'We'll never be able to thank you enough,' Dora Calloway gushed sincerely. 'You saved our boy from losing his arm. It means more to us than words can express.'

Paul felt a stab of pain within his conscience, a sudden pang of profound regret for the numerous ignorant deeds in his past. 'I'm happy the procedure worked,' he told her quietly. 'And let's hope this is the only broken bone he ever has.'

Amidst the woman's praises and thanks Paul excused himself and left the house. He was to his horse when

Jenny came up behind him.

'What? You don't even say goodbye to me?'

He kept his back to her while securing his medical bag behind the saddle. 'It wasn't my intention to snub you, Miss Calloway.'

'Let's not kick the can back and forth, Doctor Warrick,' Jenny said firmly. 'You have never explained why you were dealing faro at a casino rather than setting up shop in an office like any other doctor.'

'I'm not like any other doctor.'

He felt her hand upon his arm. 'So tell me . . . Paul,' she used his first name for the first time, 'why did you quit being a doctor?'

He gripped the saddle horn with one hand but did not climb aboard. Instead he lowered his head until it rested upon his extended arm.

'It's deeply personal, Miss Calloway, not something I can talk about to just anyone.'

'Hah!' she declared emphatically.

'That's what I am, a *just anyone* to you?'

'We aren't exactly confidential friends, nor are we involved in a courting relationship. I don't — '

'You have only yourself to blame for the fact that we aren't courting!' she snapped. 'I never thought of you as being a coward.'

Her sharp and accusing tone caused him to cock his head and look over his shoulder at her in surprise.

'Do you think I make a habit of spending endless days over here with Tom's family?' she jeered at him. 'Well, I don't. I've made a point of being here whenever you visited Billy!' She was breathing heavily from restraining a portion of her ire, her breasts rising and falling as if she had been running hard. 'Silly me,' she continued with her bitter verbal attack, 'I thought you liked me and only needed an opportunity to ask to court me!'

'I killed your cousin,' he reminded her. 'I hardly think your father would allow me to come courting.'

'You could have asked!'

Rather than defend himself he whirled around to face her. With more force and emotion than he had intended he blurted out: 'I'm not good enough for you, Jenny. Damn it all! I'm not!'

The tone and anger in his voice shocked Jenny into taking a step back. She stood dumbfounded for a moment before she could manage a response.

'I-I don't believe that,' she murmured. 'You're too good a man to have done — '

'You have no idea what I've done!' he cut off her argument.

'Then tell me!' she fired back. 'Make me understand. I want to understand. I want to know why you won't even give me a second look!'

Paul agonized over her errant conclusion. He *had* looked, and merely being close to Jenny left him mesmerized. He reached out and put his hands on her shoulders, an attempt to demonstrate in actions what he could not put into words:

'Believe me, Jenny, I want to do more than look.'

Her expression was one of confusion and supplication, a desire to comprehend his complexity while lacking the knowledge to understand his feelings. Her lips parted, as if she would speak, but there were too many questions.

Paul unconsciously moved closer, desire and a vacant yearning flooding his being. Before he could decide what to say, he impetuously drew her to him and kissed her flush on the mouth. Her reaction was swift.

She pushed against his chest with both hands and forced him back a full step. Before Paul could comprehend why he had done something so impulsive, a slap stung the side of his face, hard enough that it caused his eyes to water.

'Don't you dare!' Jenny scolded him. 'You don't have the courage to come courting but want to kiss me?' She drew back her hand as if she would strike him a second time —

'Hold it!' he said, catching hold of her wrist to ward off another blow. 'Fair's fair! One kiss, one slap!'

Jenny held the poise for a moment then jerked free and lowered her hand.

'I apologize, Miss Calloway.' He uttered a sigh. 'Really, I didn't mean to do that. I wasn't thinking straight.'

She continued to glare at him. 'I'm beginning to believe you never think straight! What's wrong with you?'

'I wanted to show you how I felt.'

'Couldn't you simply tell me that you think I'm a huckleberry above a persimmon instead of trying to go the whole hog without a word?'

He smiled at her slang. 'I've never been able to speak my mind to a woman, that's a fact.'

'You're an educated sort, a dandy from back East!'

'There are other factors involved besides knowing the right words,' he told her. 'You don't know anything about me, about my past.'

'You mean why a doctor would be dealing faro instead of helping people?'

He sighed. 'Yes, among other things.'

She softened her stance and a tight little frown furrowed her brow. 'So tell me,' she encouraged him a second time. 'I want to understand.'

Paul swallowed hard, seeking the strength to speak of his personal horrors. 'It's not something I've ever talked about, not to anyone.'

'You can tell me,' she murmured gently. 'I'd really like to know.'

'It began back when I first . . . '

Before Paul could continue, a horse and rider came thundering down the road at a hard run. He recognized Lester Calloway as the man yanked his horse to a bone jarring halt twenty feet from them. Lester jumped down from his lathered, heaving mount and threw an anxious look at Jenny.

'Where's Tom?'

'He left about an hour ago, Lester. He was going to join Buford and finish the branding. What's the matter?'

'Sheriff Roper has arrested Ken. One of Gastone's men came to your house to inform your ma. I had stopped by to pick up a part we need for our freight wagon when he arrived.'

Jenny frowned at the news. 'Why would the sheriff arrest Ken?'

'For the murder of Milo Jackson,' Lester said solemnly. 'A couple of witnesses claim they saw Ken gun the farmer down!'

'Mr Jackson has been shot and killed?'

'Sometime this morning,' Lester informed her. 'The story is that Ken and he argued over near the Ingersol place and your brother shot him dead. The sheriff caught up with Ken a couple miles from your house; his gun had been fired recently.'

'That's ridiculous!' Jenny cried. 'Ken wouldn't kill anyone. It's a lie!'

'He's been taken to jail all the same. I'm trying to locate the rest of the family to let them know.'

'Tom will be with your father over in Hay Canyon. That's where they were going to work today.'

Lester swung back up onto his horse. 'Only your ma and Sage were at your place. I'll leave it to you to pass the word to the rest of your kin.'

'I'll find Pa and Andrew,' she vowed.

Lester gave a nod of his head and kicked his horse into a run, hoofs flying as he left the yard.

Jenny turned toward the house where Dora was standing in the doorway. 'I heard what Lester said.' She spoke to Jenny and shook her head. 'I can't believe Ken would shoot one of the farmers.'

'He didn't!' Jenny maintained adamantly. 'I know he didn't.'

'I'll ride into town and see what I can find out,' Paul said, climbing aboard his horse.

'I'm going with you,' Jenny declared.

'What about notifying your father?'

'Ma will send Sage to find him and Andrew. I've got to see Ken and find out what happened. He'll tell me the truth.'

Paul waited while she retrieved her horse. Next thing they were pounding leather for town.

★   ★   ★

Dodge Roper was not at the jail. Instead Kip Hadley, the sometimes deputy, was standing guard. He stood at the door and gave Jenny a suspicious look.

'Don't try passing a gun to your brother, Miss Jenny,' he warned. 'I would hate to have to shoot him if he tried to escape.'

Jenny pulled back her riding-jacket to show she had no weapon.

'Where's the sheriff?' Paul asked.

'I'm glad you're here,' Kip replied, stepping to one side to allow Jenny to pass. As soon as she was through the door, he went on:

'The sheriff asked me to send you out to the Ingersol place. He wants you to take a look at the body before they load it in a wagon and bring it home. He is hoping you can maybe throw some light on the exact way the killing took place.'

'I'm no Pinkerton eye.'

'You're the only doctor around,' Kip responded.

'I'll trade for another horse at the livery and ride out. Better give me instructions for finding the right farm.'

Jenny partly overheard Kip asking the doctor to ride out to the scene of the shooting. However, she was more concerned with hearing what Ken had to say. He had been seated on one of the two bunks until he spied her. He leapt to his feet, came over to the cell bars and gripped them with both hands.

'Sis!' he exclaimed. 'They've got it all wrong. I didn't kill Milo Jackson.'

She stood opposite him and put both her hands on his own, offering what solace she could. 'Of course you didn't, Ken,' she assured him of her faith. 'Tell me what happened.'

'I've been meaning to shoot some rabbits for Ma lately,' he began. 'She said the other day how she wanted to fix something different for a change. Anyhow, most of the cottontail rabbits stay down near the farms.

'I got shots off at a couple but missed. You know I'm pretty good with a rifle, but not all that good with a handgun.'

'That's why your gun had been fired,' Jenny deduced. 'What about Milo Jackson?'

'I was crossing the lower end of our range when I heard a shot from the nearby farm. I thought one of the farmers might be shooting to scare off a few of our stray cattle, maybe even poaching one. I rode that way so I could have a look. Soon as I reached the edge of the farm, two farm boys started yelling at me and waving their guns. I didn't know anyone had been shot and I lit out. I guess they recognized me because the sheriff caught up with me a couple hours later and told me I was under arrest for murder.'

'Did you explain what happened?'

'Roper listened to what I had to say but those two witnesses claim they saw me after they heard the shot. I can only think I happened along right after the real killer rode off. Them two fellows seen me and thought I had done the killing.'

'Did you see anyone else?'

Ken gripped the bar until his knuckles turned white. 'I didn't see a blasted soul, Sis. But, like I said, I heard the shot and rode that way. Whoever killed Milo had time to ride off before I got there.'

'Do you think Sheriff Roper believes you?'

'I don't know. Even if he does, it won't help unless they find the real killer. I'm liable to end up in prison over this.'

'Let's not panic yet, Ken,' Jenny told her brother. 'They asked for Paul

Warrick to ride out and look over the scene. If anyone around here can figure out what happened it will be him.'

'What's to find?' Ken appeared defeated. 'I fired my gun, they have a body and two witnesses saw me fleeing on my horse.'

'Pa and Uncle Buford won't let them railroad you, Ken. You have to believe we'll be here at your side.'

Ken bobbed his head up and down in agreement, yet his shoulders drooped and he was obviously despondent. Instead of remaining at the cell door, he pulled away and returned to the bunk. Without a backward glance at Jenny, he lay down and faced the wall.

Jenny whirled about and hurried from the jail. She rushed up the street to the livery but was too late to catch up with Paul. He had already left for the Ingersol farm. She wanted to jump on her horse and catch up with him but knew it was not a good idea. At the present time she would not have been very popular with any of the farmers.

She would have to trust Paul to do his best to find evidence that would rebut the witnesses.

'Damn,' she uttered a rare profanity, 'now I wish I hadn't slapped him for kissing me!'

★　★　★

As Paul approached the huge field of corn Dodge spotted him and waved him over. Where the tilled ground ended the terrain gave way to a gentle slope, leading up to a string of choppy hills. There were a few piñon, scattered patches of sagebrush and wandering stands of tall buck-brush. Otherwise the area was fairly much open to the crests of the low-lying hills. A wagon, three saddled horses and a half-dozen men were gathered in a tight group near the main trail.

Paul rode up next to the other horses and climbed down. The sheriff came over and quickly tethered his mount for him.

'I imagine you know some of these fellows,' Dodge said, waving his hand at the group of men. 'Hal and Mac Barlow, Ernie and Vince Ingersol, Nester Gomez and Milo's cousin, Sam Jackson.'

'I'm not sure why you asked me to come out here, Sheriff.'

'We need to compile whatever evidence we can, Doc. I've never investigated an actual murder. We've had a killing or two but it was always heat of the moment and usually at the saloon.' He lifted his broad shoulders in a shrug. 'I know you are a learned man and you've probably seen a number of gunshot wounds.'

Paul didn't comment on his own qualifications or lack thereof. 'Kip said there were two witnesses,' he said.

'Mac Barlow and Vince Ingersol. They said they were in the next field over when they heard the shot. They headed over to see what happened and spotted young Ken Calloway sitting atop his horse with his gun still in his hand. They shouted at him, but Ken turned his horse and ran.'

'And they are sure it was Ken?'

'Seen him plain as day.'

'Who all has touched the body?'

'Vince said he checked to see if he there was anything they could do for Milo. When he and Mac seen he was dead Vince came to town to get me. I took a couple men out to the ranch and arrested Ken.'

Instead of approaching the body, Paul began to walk a slow circle. He studied the ground as the sheriff kept pace.

He stopped a short way from the body and did a close inspection of the ground. 'Ken was on his horse when he did the shooting?'

'That's what Vince told me,' Dodge answered. 'He claims he and Mac seen Ken atop his horse, gun in his hand, before he turned and rode off.'

'Could he tell how far away Ken was when he shot Milo?'

The sheriff paused to ask Vince the question. The answer came back: no more than fifty feet away. Armed with the information, Paul again searched the ground.

'Where did Vince get the horse for his ride to town?'

'Back at his farm. It ain't but a short way past the edge of the cornfield.'

Paul approached the body and examined the wound. The bullet had gone clear through and killed the man instantly. He looked at the entrance and exit wounds, but there was not much chance of finding the bullet. A gunsmith might have been able to determine the caliber of gun but Paul had seen Ken's pistol. It was a common make and caliber.

'What do you think, Doc?'

'I'd like to take a closer look at the body, but I'll need a table and some of my instruments.'

'We brought the wagon up here for transport,' Dodge allowed. 'We'll ship him to town so Kip can fit him with a suitable box. You can take all the time you need.'

'Let's get him loaded then. I'd like to do a more thorough examination before rigor mortis sets in.'

'Couple of you men lend a hand,' Dodge called over to the farmers. 'We're taking the body to town.'

Paul had a chance to look over the grim-faced group of men. They all appeared distressed to have lost their friend. Even so, Paul had met Ken face to face. He had heard the warmth in Jenny's voice when she talked about him. It didn't seem likely that he would shoot a man down in cold blood.

The sheriff joined Paul at his horse. 'What do you think?'

'I was told Ken's gun had been fired?'

'Yep, he claimed he was hunting rabbits a bit yonder and heard a gunshot. He said he rode over to see what was going on and Vince and Mac started pointing their fingers at him and yelling he was a killer.'

'Any reason why would they lie?'

'Not that I can think of,' Dodge

admitted ruefully. 'Plus Ken didn't have any rabbits to back up his hunting alibi.'

'He might have shot and missed at a rabbit or two.'

'He sure didn't miss Milo.'

Paul didn't want to believe Ken was a murderer but there were two witnesses who claimed to have seen him do the killing. The young man was in deep trouble.

8

The war had come to Liberty. Farmers on one side, ranchers on the other, with the town split between the two. Seth Calloway called the charge against Ken ridiculous and wanted him turned loose, while Ingersol and the other farmers demanded he stand trial for murder. Sheriff Roper contacted the US marshal's office for instruction and they wired back that a circuit judge would be dispatched.

News of the upcoming trial spread like a prairie fire. Paul was visiting Billy Calloway when Jenny arrived. Since the life or death situation had arisen, Paul had not had the chance to speak to her in private.

This didn't appear to be the right moment either. She barely looked in his direction while telling Dora the news from town.

'Jenny, dear,' Dora spoke in a gentle voice, 'we all love Ken, but are you positive he didn't do this?'

'I would bet my life on it!' Jenny avowed. 'Ken heard the shot and went to see what had happened. That's all he did.'

'Why would those two farmer boys lie about what they saw?' Paul interjected.

'I don't know,' Jenny admitted. 'Maybe they didn't get there until the real killer had ridden away, but I'm sure they are mistaken. Whoever did the shooting, it wasn't Ken.'

'The sheriff mentioned that several head of your cattle were not far from the scene,' Paul told her. 'And there were some cattle tracks in the cornfield.'

Jenny's complexion darkened and she appeared ready to rant at Paul, but Billy was standing there, wide-eyed, watching. She restrained her ire and smiled for his sake.

'We've worked hard to try and keep

the cattle away from the farms,' she said, 'but they love the corn. Sometimes they get past our riders and make their way to the farms. We do the best we can.'

Paul turned his attention to Billy and patted him on his good shoulder. 'You're doing fine, young man. Next week the splints can come off.'

'Goody!' Billy exclaimed. 'I'm real tired of having that wood wrapped around my arm.'

'We're done for today.'

Billy displayed a wide grin and ran out the door to play.

'He's had so much energy lately,' Dora spoke up, 'I worry he'll break his other arm.'

'Boys are like that,' Paul replied.

Jenny looked at Paul as if daring him to meet her gaze. He knew what was on her mind.

'You went out with the sheriff and looked at the body, Doctor Warrick,' she eventually spoke up. 'Do you think my brother killed Milo Jackson?'

'A couple witnesses say he did.'

She threw her hands in the air. 'Witnesses!' she ranted. 'Those two morons wouldn't know a snake if it crawled up and bit one of them on their nose!'

'Actually, I don't believe Ken shot Milo Jackson.' He turned to leave the room, but spoke over his shoulder to the two women. 'And I think it will be proved in a court of law.'

The frankness of his answer stunned both women. Jenny recovered quick enough to follow him out to his horse.

'What do you mean, Paul . . . ' She caught herself and quickly changed the title, 'uh, I mean, Doctor Warrick?'

He did not reply until he had removed the reins of his horse and was prepared to mount. 'Let's just say I'll volunteer to be a witness for the defense.'

'You can't leave me like this!' Jenny shouted to his back. 'What makes you think Ken didn't do the murder? What testimony can you give that will save him from prison or the gallows?'

He turned and met her frustration with a serious question. 'Are we on speaking terms again?'

'I never said I wouldn't speak to you,' she retorted testily. 'You're the one who intended to try and brand a filly without first throwing your loop.'

Her metaphor brought a grin to his lips. 'That's a good term for you — filly.'

She glowered at him and hissed the next words. 'Blast your hide, you pompous, obstinate sidewinder! Can't you be civilized and straightforward for one minute? It's not like I'm going to beat the answer out of you!'

'I'm not so certain,' he gibed. 'You slapped me pretty hard the last time we were alone.'

'You deserved it.'

'Oh, I had a slap coming, but that bruise lasted for the better part of a week.'

Jenny's teeth were clenched tightly as she fought to regain her composure.

After a lengthy internal battle she uttered a sigh.

'I'll admit that maybe I hit you harder than necessary, but I was mad at you.' She tossed her head, her hair flowing loose about her shoulders with the feminine gesture. 'It's because you . . . well, you practically showed no interest in me whatsoever. Then you take hold of me and kiss me! It made me feel wanton, as if I had asked for you to get overly . . . ' she searched for the right word and finished with: 'familiar.'

'You certainly set the record straight,' he said, pausing to rub his check. 'Might say you left an impression I won't soon forget.'

'Gads!' she exclaimed, 'men can be such babies! If it had been one of my brothers who busted you a good one for getting out of line, you would have shaken it off the next day. You hardly said a word about the beating Lester gave you.'

'Sometimes a sword to the flesh is

not nearly so devastating as a sword to the soul, Miss Calloway.'

The remark caused another tight frown. 'You're saying being slapped was more hurtful than the physical pain?'

Her perception induced him to smile. 'I knew you were an uncommonly bright young woman.'

Jenny flushed from the compliment and attempted to rebound. 'Most men aren't attracted to smart girls.'

'Only an insecure man would fear competition from a woman of wit or intellect. I have never been afraid of being bested in a debate by either sex, so long as they had a valid point of view.'

'All right, Doctor Warrick,' Jenny said after a moment, 'I apologize for striking you harder than was necessary. Does that satisfy your wounded pride?'

'Absolutely.'

'Now what about Ken? Why do you think he is innocent?'

Paul put a foot into the stirrup and prepared to climb aboard his horse. He looked back over his shoulder and said: 'Because you believe it, Miss Calloway.' Then he started to pull himself up into the saddle.

But strong hands grabbed him by the shoulders and physically restrained him. 'Not good enough!' Jenny cried. 'You're not going anywhere until . . .'

She yanked on Paul — the toe of his boot, which was still in the stirrup — swung inward and jabbed against the horse's ribs! The animal spooked and danced sideways. Paul lost hold of the saddle horn and quickly jerked his foot free from the stirrup. However, the move threw him off balance and he stumbled backward.

Jenny had both fists entwined in his shirt and could not let go. She was caught in mid-stride, unable to alter her direction or move to either side. Before she could manage an escape Paul's weight struck her, their feet tangled and they both landed on the ground.

Paul rolled over, so he would not squash the girl with his larger size, but she still had hold of his shirt. She rolled with him. Reversing direction, Paul found himself on top of her a second time, only now they were face to face.

'And you dared to call me impetuous?' he teased. 'At least I left you standing.'

'Move your carcass, you big oaf!' Jenny snapped. She placed her hands against his chest and shoved with all of her might. 'You're crushing me!'

Paul fended off Jenny's pushing by grabbing hold of her wrists and sat upright, straddling her middle. He smiled at a smudge of dirt on the end of her nose.

'Miss Calloway,' he said easily, displaying a teasing simper, 'would you be good enough to permit me to come courting?'

'Not if you were the last man on earth!' she wailed. 'Get off!'

The loudness of her voice brought Dora out to the front porch. She stopped and gaped at the scene.

'Goodness gracious me!' she cried

out. 'Whatever are you two doing?'

Paul smiled up at the woman. 'We were discussing who ought to wear the pants in a man-woman relationship. I believe I won the physical fraction of the debate.'

Jenny wrenched her hands free and shoved against his chest a second time. Paul did not resist, rising to his feet and pulling her up with him.

'Stupid horse,' Jenny explained to Dora. 'The doctor was only half-aboard when she shied away and dumped him in my lap!'

'Lucky Miss Calloway was here to catch me,' Paul said with a smirk. 'I might have suffered a nasty bruise had I landed on the hard-pack ground.'

Beginning to brush the dust off of her clothes with both hands, Jenny muttered: 'Yeah, lucky.'

Dora began to laugh.

Jenny glared at the woman but she did not stop.

'You've got dirt on the end of your nose, dear girl. However did you get your face planted in the dirt?'

Jenny jerked her thumb at Paul. 'Ask him,' she replied sourly. 'He was on top.'

Deciding he had done enough damage to his relationship with Jenny for one day, Paul dusted himself off and mounted his horse. He paused to tip his hat and smiled one last time.

'Always nice to visit with you ladies,' he said. Looking at Dora, 'I'll be back next week to remove the splints and check Billy's arm one last time.' She gave a nod and wave.

'As for you, Genevieve Calloway, I'll be waiting to hear back from you concerning my proposal.'

Jenny's face flushed crimson and her lips pressed into a thin line. Paul was smart enough not to ask for her answer at that moment. He left as quickly as his horse could be turned for the main trail.

Even before he was out of earshot he heard Dora ask Jenny: 'What proposal is he talking about and what were you two really up to rolling around on the ground?' A pause, then: 'Jenny? Jenny, answer me!'

Paul could not help but chuckle at the situation.

'Paul, old boy, you definitely made an impression on that young lady. Lucky you didn't break her neck!'

★ ★ ★

Ernie stood before the usual leaders of the farmers' faction. Hal Barlow and Nester Gomez, along with Sam Jackson who had replaced his cousin.

'My son was snooping around town and overheard a couple of cowboys talking. One of them said that the doctor feller figured his testimony could sure enough get Ken off at trial.'

'That don't make sense,' Sam growled the words. 'Your boy and Mac done seen Ken riding away from the killing. How can that Warrick fellow prove it didn't happen exactly the way the boys seen it?'

'The gent is one slippery son,' Hal spoke up. 'He kills Ned like a hired gun, but then turns out to be a doctor and saves the sheriff's daughter and her baby all in the same night.'

'Don't forget Billy Calloway,' Nester contributed. 'Saved his arm, so the story goes. Bone was stickin' out, busted so bad it looked as if the only way to save the boy's life was to amputate. Then Warrick steps in and saves the day.' He shook his head. 'I tell you, that man is about as big a puzzle as the one about which came first, the chicken or the egg.'

Ernie waved a hand to dismiss the chatter. 'I'm telling you men, this is our chance to take control. We put Ken behind bars for killing poor Milo in cold blood and no one will even question our right to string wire to protect our crops.'

'You maybe got a point,' Hal admitted, 'but why would Warrick claim he could get Ken off. My boy backs up every word your son says about the shooting, Ernie. Ken shot Milo dead and everyone knows Milo never carried a gun. So I'm wondering what the doc could possibly say that would change how any judge or jury would vote?'

'I'm telling you what Vince over-heard,' Ernie replied. 'I don't have any idea what the man is going to say, but he's proved to be up to every task given him. I, for one, am not going to sit by and let a killer walk away free.'

'We can't get into a shooting war with the Calloway bunch,' Hal was quick to point out. 'They would cut us down like a handful of weeds standing against a sharpened hoe.'

'Besides which we want the people in town on our side,' Nester said. 'We go gunning for Ken and it will be taking the law into our own hands.'

Before anyone else could speak up, Ernie held up both hands, palms out. 'Hold on, men,' he soothed them with a calm voice. 'I have the answer.'

'So speak up,' Hal prodded him. 'What's the plan?'

'My uncle knows this man in Cheyenne, he's a big-time lawyer, see?' At the curious look from the others, he continued: 'We need to pool our money.'

★   ★   ★

Paul left the café and stepped out into the evening air. All that remained of the sun was a soft glow along the western horizon. The breeze stirred his hat and a dust devil touched down and spun crazily along between the buildings for a short way before vanishing.

A number of people were moving around, it being a Saturday night. A few men were passing by on horseback, a couple wagons rolled along the street and others were standing and talking or simply passing the time. He returned the wave from a couple familiar faces from Mort Gastone's casino. He should have known their names but he never did a lot of socializing.

Paul began walking toward his hotel,

weaving along through the traffic. He heard his name called, stopped and turned in nearly the same motion.

At that instant a shot rang out.

Not since the war had a bullet gone past his ear close enough for him to hear it. He ducked instinctively as the report echoed through the dusk. At nearly the same time Kip Hadley grunted from the bullet striking him at the top of his shoulder.

Men shouted and ran from every direction, drawn to the street at hearing the gunshot. One man thought the gun had been fired from a nearby alley, so several men went looking for the shooter. Paul made his way over to Kip and led him over to the porch. Once he was sitting down, Paul inspected the wound.

'Made a nice little furrow across the top of your shoulder but missed the bone. Not much more than a deep scratch.'

Kip gave his head a shake. 'What the hell, Doc? Ain't no way someone would shoot at me. I ain't got an enemy in the world.'

Paul looked across the street, staring at the spot where one of the men thought they had seen a muzzle-flash from the shooter. Kip was right. The bullet wasn't meant for him. A sudden chill encased his spine and caused him to shiver.

'Come over to the hotel and I'll put a bandage on that for you.'

Kip cocked his head so he could see the graze. 'Shucks, it ain't hardly bleeding none. Getting grazed by the slug was more surprise than pain.'

'Did you call my name?' Paul asked.

'Yeah, I fixed up them two old Injun arrows like you asked. Whatever are you going to do with them?'

'They are for a demonstration, Kip. I'll probably need you to help me . . . providing your shoulder doesn't bother you.'

'Like I said, it don't hardly hurt none.' He flexed the shoulder as if to prove his point. 'Whatever you need,

Doc, I'm your man.'

'Come over to my room. I still want to clean and bandage the wound. No need to risk infection.'

'Sure enough,' Kip said. 'Might as well baby the tiny scratch. It could be the only gunshot wound I ever get.'

It didn't take much to treat Kip's injury. He was out of Paul's room in five minutes . . . just in time for Dodge Roper to arrive. Kip and Dodge exchanged a few words in the hallway, as the sheriff wanted an update on his condition. After their conversation, Dodge pushed open Paul's door. His voice was gruff.

'Warrick, what the hell have you been up to?'

Paul feigned innocence. 'Me? I've been right here patching up Kip's wound. It wasn't much more than a scratch.'

'And where were you when the shooting took place?'

'I was out on the street.'

Dodge rolled his eyes. 'So someone

183

shot at you and hit Kip. I knew it was something like that.'

'You are jumping to conclusions, Sheriff.'

'Tell me I'm wrong,' he challenged. 'Go ahead, tell me why anyone would take a shot at Kip!'

'You think I'm the one they were shooting at?'

'We both know the answer to that question,' Dodge told him. 'Word has gotten around how you think Ken is innocent. I'd say there are a number of people who are more than a little upset by that news.' He narrowed his gaze. 'I can think of one in particular — the actual killer himself!'

'You mean to tell me you've decided you have an innocent man locked up in jail?'

'I don't know you real well, Warrick, but I darn sure know you are not a man given to exaggerations. If you say you can prove Ken is innocent, I'll be taking your word for it.'

'Never knew my word to count for

that much before,' Paul said. 'Makes me feel kind of humble, honored even.'

'Yeah, well, I don't intend to be honoring you at a funeral service! I've a mind to put you into custody again, lock you in a jail cell until the judge arrives.'

'Whoever took the shot ran like a spooked jackrabbit, Sheriff. I don't think he'll try a second time.'

'There are a number of farmers in this valley, Doc. Some of them might be better shots than the one who tried to get you down on the street.'

'If I was a farmer, I'd want the real killer of Milo Jackson. I'm pretty sure I know who that is.'

Dodge leaned closer. 'You know who killed Milo?' he asked softly, as if fearful someone might overhear. 'You ain't guessing, you really know?'

'I would like you to do me a favor, Sheriff,' Paul did not answer the sheriff's question directly. 'When we have the formal hearing, I want you to make everyone leave their guns outside, no weapons of any kind in the courtroom other than for you. Can you do that?'

'You expecting a riot to break out?'

Paul shrugged. 'If I point a finger at someone and call him a murderer, I don't want him able to draw his gun and kill me on the spot. Neither would I care to have a range war break out in the courtroom at that very moment. You need to have control of the situation before it gets out of hand.'

'I can do that,' Dodge maintained. 'I'll deputize a couple of men, have them posted by the door.' He snorted. 'I'll have old Bess and her twin loads of buckshot handy too. I can be real persuasive with that shotgun in my hands.'

'Good.'

'But until the judge arrives, you stay close. No taking rides out to see your gal. Anyone needs a doctor they can darn well come into town. Them's my rules!'

'I'll do my best to abide by them, Sheriff.'

Dodge gave a nod. 'I'm going to pass the word to the livery. You'll have to steal a horse to get out of town.'

'I understand.'

Dodge gave a tug on his hat, as if the matter was settled. 'I'll see you around.'

Paul watched him go and heaved a sigh. He hoped it wouldn't be too long before the judge arrived. He wanted to get this behind him.

9

Two weeks to the day after Ken was jailed, a circuit judge arrived in town. The farmers had put together their money and hired a prosecuting attorney from Cheyenne. Nathan Cole was known for his prowess in the court-room, seldom losing a case.

Paul had been sleeping better but last night the dreams came again to haunt him, flooding his brain with images of gore, agony and the sheer horror of his own existence. Still a bit red-eyed, with a dull ache in his head, he was up, washed and shaved shortly after sun-up. He donned fresh clothing and put together a bundle for the laundry.

Before he had finished a knock came at his door. He set aside the dirty clothes and opened the door. He had not seen Jenny since pinning her to the ground at Tom's place. He was a bit surprised to discover her standing in the hallway.

'Miss Calloway?'

'I need to talk to you,' she said. Then without waiting to be invited she stepped into the room.

'Do come in . . . said the fox to the baby chick,' he said, displaying a grin as he closed the door.

She ignored his levity. 'You've heard about the prosecutor, the one the farmers hired?'

'Sheriff Roper told me about him. It's rumored he is very good.'

Jenny spun about to look at him. She wore a denim riding skirt, snug cotton blouse and a lady's Stetson was atop her head. Worry lines creased her otherwise flawless face and there was a silent plea in her eyes.

'I've spoken to everyone in town and no one has offered to defend my brother.'

'I thought perhaps Bryan . . . '

She gave her head a negative toss. 'I asked him if he would but he doesn't think he can win against a professional. He's never even been to a real court trial.'

The purpose of her visit was now clear to Paul. 'And you want me to defend Ken.' It was a statement, not a question.

'You told me that you believed he was innocent,' she pounced on his remark. 'At Tom's place, when you . . .' she hesitated, 'when I last saw you,' she finished.

'I'm not qualified to represent your brother. I will testify on his behalf, but . . .'

Jenny moved toward him, standing close enough for him to detect the scent of the perfumed soap that she had used on her hair. The plea formed on her exquisite mouth as her gaze turned Paul's resolve into dust.

'Please, Paul,' she murmured softly. 'I have no one else to turn to. You are Ken's best hope.'

'It doesn't matter whether the farmers have a genuine prosecutor,' Paul protested. 'My testimony should be enough to set him free.'

'I've never been to a real trial, but I've read of some cases and know the truth is not always enough.'

Paul firmed his resolve. 'I won't be tricked or dubbed by some shifty lawyer's double-talk, Jenny. You'll have to take my word for it.'

Jenny stepped in close and placed her hands on his shoulders. 'I want to believe you, Paul, I do.' Her eyes were searching, probing, seducing his will. 'But how can you be so certain? What do you know that will save him?'

'I need you to trust me.'

Jenny let go and whirled about, turning her back to him. 'You ask me to trust you, but this is all your fault.'

'My fault?'

'You killed Ned. It's what started all of the trouble in the valley.'

'I thought you understood about Ned.'

She spun back around, eyes ablaze. 'I understand you had to shoot him, but tell me, *Doctor*,' her voice turned accusing and harsh, 'why were you dealing faro? Why does a doctor quit his profession and turn to gambling for a living?'

'I wasn't gambling,' he said defensively. 'I was working for Gastone. Dealing faro was a job, nothing more.'

'That doesn't explain why you quit your doctoring. Why give up a noble profession for the smoke, monotony and horrible hours of working a table at a casino?'

Paul could not meet her intense stare. He started to turn away from her, but Jenny caught hold of his shoulders and dug her fingers into his flesh.

'What are you hiding from me?' she demanded know. 'You kissed me, you asked if you could court me, I have a right to know!'

'You slapped me for the kiss and never consented to the courting,' he argued back. 'I don't see that you have earned any special right to know anything about me.'

'All right!' she fired at him. 'Here!'

And with that peremptory word she pulled him to her and planted her lips on his. More than a mere kiss, the heated contact was a torrid fusion, a volcano about to erupt. She wrapped her arms about him, engulfing him with the smoldering fire of her unleashed passion.

Paul struggled to maintain his composure as he felt he might collapse into a trembling heap at Jenny's feet. He had never been so completely overwhelmed in his life. To counter her fantastic assault, he summoned the only riposte he could think of — he must kiss her back.

By the time his manly defenses had mustered forth the strength to match Jenny's feverish ardor she had pulled out of his grasp.

They stood there like two dummies, each staring at the other with a perplexed amazement. Calling forth what remnants of willpower he could, Paul managed to find a steadiness in his voice as he spoke to Jenny.

'I don't recall what the argument was about,' he announced easily, 'but I readily agree with your point of view.'

Jenny's cheeks were pink with chagrin. 'I-I didn't . . . ' she gasped, still struggling to catch her breath. 'I wasn't trying to . . . to . . . '

'You needn't apologize,' Paul told her.

Jenny's small hands balled into fists, arms rigid at her sides. 'I was not going to apologize,' she snapped. 'You won't open up to me. You're hiding something and I want to know what it is!'

'So it was planned coercion, kissing me?' He gave his head a shake. 'We could have used you during the war to interrogate prisoners.'

She did not smile at his attempted humor. 'I kissed you so you would again be beholden to me. You said the slap removed any previous debt between us. Unless you wish to slap my face for being so impudent, you again owe me something.'

'I could kiss you and call it even?'

'Durn your ornery hide, Paul!' She grated the words. 'Tell me the truth!'

Rather than reply or prolong the inevitable Paul moved over to the bed and sat down. Wordlessly, Jenny came over and sat at his side. She did not prod, waiting for him to confess his deep dark secret.

'We were at Vicksburg,' he began, thinking back to the most ghastly night of his life. 'The battle between the Union and Confederate forces raged for hours with each side advancing and retreating along several fronts. We needed a hospital for the wounded and commandeered a large manor.'

He paused recalling the stately home and how he had hated to destroy the lives of those within by turning it into a field hospital.

'Most of the workers had deserted the place, all of the animals were gone, except for a kitten, and there wasn't a bite of food in the house. The men who had lived on the estate were off fighting in the war so there was only a woman and her three children — two boys, maybe eight and nine years old, along with a little girl of about four — still in the house. The woman protested at first, but when she saw the condition of our wounded and suffering she had a change of heart. She sent her kids to their room and offered to help with some of the injured.

'The battle took a turn for the worse and our lines retreated until we were in the middle of the fighting. Cannon fire rocked the house and we decided we would have to move the wounded back to safer ground.'

Paul stopped speaking, the memory still horrific and vivid. He envisioned the screaming men and the hacking off of limbs to stop excessive bleeding or shattered bones. The medical supplies were exhausted and most of the patients suffered incredible agony until they passed out from the pain. The gore was ubiquitous, the mangled bodies, the stench of blood and the wails and moaning of those wounded, dead or dying were harrowing beyond belief.

Sucking in a breath he summoned his courage and went on with the tale.

'The noise of gunfire and the explosions from cannons shook the house and frightened the kitten. When someone opened the front door it ran outside.' Paul swallowed hard to keep his voice from cracking. Jenny's hand slid over to rest on his own, a silent encouragement to finish his story. 'The little girl was afraid for the kitten so she ignored her mother's warning shout and ran outside too.'

He closed his eyes, pinching the lids to stave off tears. 'A soldier brought the child in a few minutes later. She had been hit by shrapnel.' He again swallowed hard. 'The mother was hysterical and had to be dragged from the room. I tried to stop the bleeding, but the damage . . . '

It took a full minute and several deep breaths before he could continue. 'That precious little girl, while dying in front of me, looked up at me with a desperate plea in her eyes. She must have known her life was nearly gone, yet she didn't think of herself. She whispered, 'Mister, please find my kitty,' then she closed her eyes. I watched, completely helpless, as that tiny, beautiful soul departed from this earth. All she knew of the world was the ugliness of war and a world of hate and bloodshed . . . other than her love for her kitten.'

Jenny suffered the sorrowful tale in silence a short while before at last she looked at Paul. A sob lodged in her throat and tears wet her cheeks.

'The death of that little girl severed the last string which had been holding my sanity together,' Paul concluded. 'I saw myself for what I'd become — no longer a respectable surgeon, but a backyard butcher, sawing off limbs and stuffing rags into gaping holes to slow the blood-loss. More than a butcher, I had become an earthly god, taking a single look at a man and deciding whether he could be saved or carted off and left to die. I committed dozens of men to death who might have survived, had I been given the time to bind or treat their wounds properly. No mortal person is equipped to live with those decisions.'

Paul pinched his eyes shut a second time, trying to shut out the horrid visions. Perhaps speaking of the pain actually helped as he found his voice to finish the story.

'The sheer number of the victims has haunted me to this day. I see the face of that little girl and a thousand of the soldiers' mutilated bodies every time I close my eyes. I see a mountain of limbs, amputations I now know were unnecessary. I recall the unholy terror in the eyes of the wounded, the blood and gore, the inherent savagery and brutality of man's inhumanity to man. To save what little was left of my mind, I took the coward's way out. As soon as the battle ended I resigned and headed west. I've been running from my past ever since that night.'

'You did what you had to do,' Jenny murmured. 'You can't run away from your memories. You need to forgive yourself for something over which you had no control.' She took hold of his hand and squeezed it between her own. 'You didn't start the war that killed over a half-million men and you didn't kill that little girl. Like the rest of our countrymen you were a victim of the war.'

When Paul did not respond Jenny leaned over and kissed him tenderly on the lips. It was not passion, but compassion, an understanding and sharing of his pain. When she pulled back she smiled.

'And you saved Sarah and Paulette's lives,' she reminded him. 'Plus Billy has two arms thanks to you. I'd say you have been doing your share of good deeds since you arrived at Liberty.'

'You left out my killing Ned.'

'When you successfully defend my brother and prove he didn't murder Milo Jackson, I think even Buford will agree the debt is paid.'

'Maybe I'll make a terrible lawyer.'

'I don't believe that,' she quipped. 'I don't think there is anything you can't do, once you put your mind to it.'

Paul looked at her and felt a renewed strength. 'When I was at college, I shared a room with a guy who was going to law school. He told me the key to winning a case was to figure out who was the guilty party. Then you only had to ask the right questions.'

'It sounds simple.'

'Yes, if everyone who took the witness stand told the truth. I'm pretty sure that won't be the case tomorrow.'

'You told me you could prove Ken's innocence!'

'Maybe I only made the boast because I was trying to impress a pretty girl.'

She smiled. 'Not that I think you are above such underhanded tricks, but I think you were telling the truth. You know something.'

'Maybe.'

'Something that nearly got you killed,' she added. 'I heard about the shooting.'

'Probably a drunk firing off a round at a pink elephant.'

Jenny fixed her brows tightly together. 'A pink elephant?'

'Too much drink can give some people hallucinations.'

'Will you defend my brother?'

Paul had already supposed he would be doing most of Ken's defense work, so taking on the chore of his lawyer was not going to be difficult. Of course, withholding his answer might be worth a little something extra.

'I'll do it for a proper fee,' he said. Shock sprang into Jenny's face, until he added: 'One more good kiss.'

Jenny's expression softened at once, but a mischievous light danced in her eyes. 'You know, Paul,' she murmured, pausing to moisten her lips with a flick of her tongue, 'you have bypassed all of the *courting* rules and moved right to the *sparking* of our relationship. If I was to tell my pa and brothers about this, they might insist on the two of us getting married.'

Paul smiled. 'You tell them anything you want, Jenny. If they demand I be a man of honor, I'll sure enough do my duty.'

'I'm not altogether sure I want to be considered *your duty*!'

Rather than wait for her to make the next advance, Paul initiated an offensive of his own, drawing her into his arms and kissing her. She felt warm, pliant and loving in his embrace, just what he needed to blot out the morbid memories of his past.

10

Nathan Cole possessed an eloquent manner of speaking and asked direct and purposeful questions. He put two farmers on the witness stand to demonstrate the conflict between them and the ranchers. Next he questioned Dodge Roper about Ken's gun being fired and brought out the fact that Ken admitted to having been at the murder site. In an odd twist, he also asked Paul to take the stand. His single question was only to confirm that the man's death was due to a single gunshot wound. With motive and opportunity proven, he played his high card and put Vince Ingersol on the stand to state what he had seen.

All through the proceedings Paul remained silent. He asked no questions of any of the witnesses but did ask that they should remain available to be recalled for the defense. When Nathan finished with Vince he called Mac Barlow to back up his story. Mac repeated the account of the event as told by Vince roughly verbatim. When he had finished with the man's testimony he turned away from the witness chair.

'The prosecution rests,' Nathan announced to the judge, took his chair and flashed a confident smile at the men who had hired him. He had built a strong case against Ken.

It was common knowledge that Mac was a little slow when it came to thinking on his own and Paul had noticed how he looked to Vince for approval after every answer. He knew Mac would be his best chance to break under pressure and unlock the truth.

'Mac Barlow, you have testified under oath,' he began, looking directly into his eyes. 'Are you a religious man?'

'Uh . . . yes, sir, I sure am,' replied Mac. 'I don't hardly never miss a Sunday meeting.'

'Then you must be aware of the Ten Commandments?'

'I know all about them,' he replied.

Nathan rose from his chair. 'Is there a question here that is relevant to the case before the court?'

The judge looked at Paul for an answer.

'I need to ascertain the moral fiber of this witness,' Paul explained. 'I want him to be aware of his moral responsibility to tell the complete truth.'

'Proceed,' the judge said, 'but let's move on with the questioning.'

'You testified that you and Vince heard the shot which killed Milo Jackson, is that correct?'

'Yes, sir.'

'And you were in the next field approximately a hundred yards away?'

'Yup.'

'When you spotted Ken, he had his gun out and Milo had fallen to the ground mortally wounded. And you are certain he shot and killed Milo while mounted on the back of his horse.'

206

Mac flicked a quick glance at Vince and then bobbed his head up and down. 'Yup, that's just the way it happened.'

'Ken couldn't have shot Milo from the ground and then got on his horse?'

Mac sneaked another glance at Vince. 'No,' he stated confidently, 'he didn't have time for that. We looked up right after the shot was fired.'

Paul turned to the judge. 'With the court's permission, I should like to give a quick demonstration. It will have a direct bearing on this man's testimony.'

'Very well,' the judge said. 'I'll allow it.'

Kip came forward carrying the two trimmed arrows he had prepared for Paul. He moved between Mac and Vince and stopped a couple feet in front of the witness stand. Awaiting instructions, he stood like a soldier at attention, holding himself as erect and rigid as he could.

'A man shooting from the back of a horse would be about the equivalent to my standing on a chair,' Paul explained, pulling a chair over and stepping up onto it. He rose up, extended his arm and pointed at Kip, using his finger like a gun. 'That would put Ken about like this and Kip would be Milo.' He paused to look at Mac. 'Wouldn't you agree?'

Mac gave a shrug.

'Right about there, Kip,' Paul directed.

Kip held the flat of the arrow shaft to his chest and slid it to the side and tucked it under his left armpit. With Paul urging up a little higher or lower, he tilted the arrow until the alignment was correct.

'As you can see by the shaft of the arrow,' he spoke to Mac, while stepping down from his chair, 'the bullet would enter fairly high in the chest and have a lower exit wound from his back. Can you see that?'

Mac tried to get a look at Vince, but Kip blocked his view. He gave an uncertain bob of his head and agreed: 'Yeah, I guess so.'

'A man on foot would shoot at an

even plane, providing the ground was fairly level — and it was level at the spot where Milo was killed.' He aimed a second time and Kip placed the second arrow against his chest, holding it with his right hand to show a direct path though the body.

'Quite a difference isn't it, Mac?' Paul asked.

'Yup, reckon it is.'

'I want you to study the second shaft, Mac,' Paul pointed at the nearly horizontal arrow. 'When I examined the body, I found that was the trail the bullet took through Milo Jackson. There is no doubt he was shot by someone standing on the ground.'

Paul took a step toward Mac and pointed his finger at him. 'You testified Ken fired from the back of his horse, but there were no hoof prints within a hundred feet of Milo's body! Secondly, the path of the bullet indicates he was shot by someone on the ground. Ken couldn't have shot Milo from the back of his horse!'

Mac cowered from the verbal assault.

'What really happened, Mac?' Paul asked harshly. 'Was Milo killed because of the barbed wire? Was it because Milo opposed the wire?'

Mac began to turn his head from side to side, his face a mask of confusion.

'Did you shoot Milo? Is that what happened?'

'No!' he cried. 'I didn't shoot — '

'And what about me?' Paul demanded. 'Was it you who took the shot at me out in the street? Did you want to kill me so I couldn't tell the truth about Milo's murder here today?'

'No . . . no!' The big man looked ready to cry. 'It wasn't me!'

'The Ten Commandments, Mac,' Paul continued to drill him with a verbal barrage. 'It says 'thou shalt not bear false witness against thy neighbor'. Do you know what that means?'

Mac could no longer speak. He gave his head a violent shake.

'You are a witness here today, Mac. The Commandments say you must tell the truth or God will punish you. Do you understand now?'

Penny-sized tears slid down Mac's cheeks. He searched the room for help and guidance, but Kip continued to stand between him and Vince.

Hal Barlow suddenly stood up. 'Tell the truth, son!' he ordered. 'Milo was our neighbor and friend. You damn well better tell us how he died!'

'Vince!' Mac cried out. 'Tell me what to say, Vince. I . . . I don't know what to do!'

Vince started to rise but Dodge was there to put a gun against his ribs. 'It took some searching,' he told the young man, his voice loud enough for everyone in the room to hear, 'but I found a witness who saw you ride into town a few minutes before someone took a shot at the doctor. I figure you didn't want him to bring out the truth today.'

'Vincent!' Ernie wailed, also jumping to his feet. 'Tell me you didn't do this!'

'Milo wouldn't listen.' Vince sneered

back at him. 'You kept telling me how he was holding up the wire. He wouldn't listen to reason.'

'But he had!' Ernie said sorrowfully. 'He was going to go along with the wire once I had enough people supporting us. No one had to die!'

The judge banged his gavel to get everyone's attention. 'It is quite obvious we have the wrong man in custody here. I'm ruling that Ken Calloway is not guilty of murder and will expect formal charges to be brought against this other young man. This court is adjourned until such time as we can set up a new hearing.'

Dodge and Kip escorted Vince and Mac to jail.

Ernie remained seated, crushed by the turn of events. He didn't look up until Seth Calloway planted his large frame in front of him.

'What about this wire?' he asked.

'We wanted to fence the crops to keep the cattle out,' Ernie explained. 'We were going to leave a pathway open between each farm so the cattle could still get to the creek for water.'

Seth put a hand on his shoulder. 'I think we can work something out that will work for us both, Ingersol. When your wire arrives, let us know and we'll send some men to help.'

Ernie nodded, still crestfallen that his son had murdered their neighbor and friend, then attempted to frame an innocent man. Worse, he had also tried to kill the doctor to keep him from testifying.

'God forgive me,' he muttered. 'I should have told Vince about our new plan. There was no need for anyone to get hurt.'

Paul shook hands with Ken and was mobbed by the entire Calloway clan. When two arms came around his chest and a soft body pressed against him from behind, he looked over his shoulder to discover Jenny clinging to him like a second shadow.

'You gonna' ask my pa for permission to come courting or do I have to get rough with you?'

Seth had finished speaking to Ernie and overheard her question. He gave Paul a long hard look. 'Don't know if you're man enough to handle her, Warrick, but we'd all be happy as hell to be rid of her.'

Some of the other Calloway clan laughed. Even Buford smiled.

'I'll be first to admit,' he said, 'hitching your wagon to Jenny would be a fair penance for killing my son.'

'Yes!' Jenny laughed. 'A *lifelong* sentence!'

'I'd be honored if you would allow me to court your daughter, Mr Calloway,' Paul said to Seth. 'I only hope I'm good enough for her.'

Ken edged forward and put on a stern expression. 'Oh, I think you'll be good.'

Tom joined Ken with Lester and Andrew at his side. 'Durn right you'll be good!' he declared. 'We'll all be watching every move you make.'

'Well,' Ken relaxed to grin, 'maybe

not every move.'

Jenny slid around to Paul's front and kissed him on the lips. When she pulled back the mischievous fires were aflame and dancing in her eyes. 'He kissed me right here in public, Pa,' she announced. 'You seen it for yourself. Now he's got to marry me!'

Paul laughed at her ambush. He hadn't really laughed in a long time. Jenny truly was the answer he had been searching for these past years. Slipping his arms around her, he pulled her close.

'I believe a honeymoon trip to Denver and a night at the theater ought to be just what the doctor ordered,' he said.

Jenny uttered a girlish cry and kissed him a second time. Paul relished holding her tight and knew he no longer had to run from his nightmares. The good woman in his arms would help him to find a lasting peace of mind.

We do hope that you have enjoyed reading this large print book.

Did you know that all of our titles are available for purchase?

We publish a wide range of high quality large print books including:
Romances, Mysteries, Classics
General Fiction
Non Fiction and Westerns

Special interest titles available in large print are:
The Little Oxford Dictionary
Music Book, Song Book
Hymn Book, Service Book

Also available from us courtesy of Oxford University Press:
Young Readers' Dictionary
(large print edition)
Young Readers' Thesaurus
(large print edition)

For further information or a free brochure, please contact us at:
Ulverscroft Large Print Books Ltd.,
The Green, Bradgate Road, Anstey,
Leicester, LE7 7FU, England.
Tel: (00 44) **0116 236 4325**
Fax: (00 44) **0116 234 0205**

MASSACRE AT BLUFF POINT

I. J. Parnham

Ethan Craig has only just started working for Sam Pringle's outfit when Ansel Stark's bandits bushwhack the men at Bluff Point. Ethan's new colleagues are gunned down in cold blood and he vows revenge. But Ethan's manhunt never gets underway — Sheriff Henry Fisher arrests him and he's accused of being a member of the very gang he'd sworn to track down! With nobody believing his innocence and a ruthless bandit to catch, can Ethan ever hope to succeed?